Falling for the Single Dad

Lisa Carter

HARLEQUIN® LOVE INSPIRED®

If you purchased this book without a cover you should be aware that this book is stolen property. It was reported as "unsold and destroyed" to the publisher, and neither the author nor the publisher has received any payment for this "stripped book."

Recycling programs
for this product may
not exist in your area.

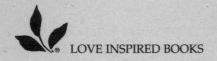 LOVE INSPIRED BOOKS

ISBN-13: 978-0-373-81933-1

Falling for the Single Dad

Copyright © 2016 by Lisa Carter

All rights reserved. Except for use in any review, the reproduction or utilization of this work in whole or in part in any form by any electronic, mechanical or other means, now known or hereinafter invented, including xerography, photocopying and recording, or in any information storage or retrieval system, is forbidden without the written permission of the editorial office, Love Inspired Books, 195 Broadway, New York, NY 10007 U.S.A.

This is a work of fiction. Names, characters, places and incidents are either the product of the author's imagination or are used fictitiously, and any resemblance to actual persons, living or dead, business establishments, events or locales is entirely coincidental.

This edition published by arrangement with Love Inspired Books.

® and TM are trademarks of Love Inspired Books, used under license. Trademarks indicated with ® are registered in the United States Patent and Trademark Office, the Canadian Intellectual Property Office and in other countries.

www.Harlequin.com

Printed in U.S.A.

Let us hold unswervingly to the hope we profess,
for he who promised is faithful.
—*Hebrews* 10:23

Dedicated to David and Peggy Riley

You advised me long ago to read a psalm a day, and you were right. Thanks for your friendship and support. You two make a great team. Yours is a special gift, a noble legacy—to shine the Light. Your example of godly leadership has been a beacon of light and truth to me throughout the years.

Acknowledgments

Thanks to Kathy Davis for her quick, on-the-scene guidance regarding the exact layout of the bridge, the tunnels and the pier at the Chesapeake Grill at the exact minute I was trying to write that scene. Any errors are, of course, my own.

The Virginia Institute of Marine Science (VIMS) is real. Its three-part mission is "to conduct interdisciplinary research in coastal ocean and estuarine science, educate students and citizens, and provide advisory service to policy makers, industry, and the public." I've taken a few liberties with the actual facility layout. And currently, no marine rescue/rehabilitation/ conservation center exists on the Virginia portion of the Delmarva Peninsula. But wouldn't it be fun if such a place did?

Chapter One

"Excuse me? Excuse…meeee…?"

Startled, Caroline Duer gazed to the left, then right, before coming to rest on the heart-shaped face of a little girl tugging on her sleeve. "Were you talking to me?"

The child's shoulder-length tangle of red hair bobbed as she nodded. "Would you help me find a book?"

Her enormous blue eyes inspected Caroline for a second. And as if an afterthought, she added, "Please."

Caroline's eyes skittered around the Kiptohanock Library. "Um…"

Moments before, a librarian had been reading to a cluster of children on the big green rug. Obviously, one of her charges had wandered.

"I don't see her right now, but…"

Where was a librarian when you needed one?

"Uh…" Caroline wasn't good with children. Sea creatures, yes. Little girls, no.

This was what happened when you put off what needed to be done. You got roped into over-your-head situations.

"I'm not—"

"But I said the special word." The little girl cocked her head and waited.

Special word? What in the name of fried flounder was a special word? A secret children's language to which Caroline wasn't privy? "I'm sorry, dear…"

The little girl scowled.

"Dear" must not be a special word. Where was the librarian? Caroline cut her eyes over to the child.

The little redhead planted her fist on her hip. And jutted it. "I need *you.*"

Just Caroline's luck. A tyke with attitude.

The little girl *needed* her? A clear case of mistaken identity, but it had been a long time since anyone needed her. In fact, the last time she'd been needed, she'd failed everyone so completely.

She was perhaps the worst person on earth anyone needed to need. Caroline swallowed. Where was the librarian? Better yet, where was this child's mother?

Even Caroline understood children required a lot of time. More time than she as a thirty-five-

"Caroline could take me shopping."

He reddened. "Izzie, I'm sure the lady vet is busy. She probably has much more—"

"I'd love to take Izzie shopping." Caroline gave him a defiant look. "Why don't you bring her to the animal rescue center later this week—say Thursday—about four o'clock?"

Izzie bounced on the balls of her feet. "Yay!"

"You don't need to—"

"And you're welcome." Caroline slipped behind the wheel.

His lips quirked. "Like you said yesterday, I'm sure I would've managed somehow, but…" He rolled his tongue in his cheek.

"Is that your idea of a thank-you?" She laughed. "Not much of a people person, are you?"

Weston leaned his elbows against the car window. "Will you allow me to fix dinner after you and Izzie return from your shopping expedition? I could give you a tour of our home-slash-work-in-progress."

She smiled at him. "I'd like that. Till then?"

Till then. His mouth went dry. Had he lost what little mind he still possessed? What had he done?

Lisa Carter and her family make their home in North Carolina. In addition to her Love Inspired novels, she writes romantic suspense for Abingdon Press. When she isn't writing, Lisa enjoys traveling to romantic locales, teaching writing workshops and researching her next exotic adventure. She has strong opinions on barbecue and ACC basketball. She loves to hear from readers. Connect with Lisa at lisacarterauthor.com.

Books by Lisa Carter

Love Inspired

Coast Guard Courtship
Coast Guard Sweetheart
Falling for the Single Dad

year-old marine veterinarian was willing to pencil into her schedule. If you couldn't spare the time, don't have 'em. She drummed her restless fingers on the wooden surface of the librarian's desk.

"I want books like that." The little girl pointed at the illustrated Eastern Shore bird-watcher's field guide in Caroline's hand. "Books about turtles and dolphins, too."

Caroline glanced from the book to the little girl. "This is a book my sister, Amelia, illustrated. Illustrated means—"

"She drew the pictures." The little girl fluttered her hand as if shooing sand fleas. "I know all about that."

Caroline's lips twitched. Okay, the redhead was a *smart* little girl.

"Are you going to check it out?"

"I don't live around here." Caroline's gaze darted out the window overlooking the Kiptohanock square. "Not anymore. I don't have a library card."

The little girl dug a plastic card out of the pocket of her jeans. "I do." She held up the card. "I've had my own library card since I learned to read when I was four. My daddy says I'm a reading machine."

Caroline stifled a laugh. The same could've

been said of her as a child, too. She passed the book into the little girl's custody.

The redhead grinned at Caroline. "Thanks."

Caroline shifted to move past her. "You're welcome."

"Aren't you going to help me find the book on turtles?"

Caroline studied the expectant little face. "You're not going to leave me alone till I do, are you?"

The little girl smiled. Tiny lines feathered the corners of her eyes. An indication she was a happy child? Caroline hoped so.

"All right. Come on, then." Racking her brain for what she remembered of the Dewey Decimal System, Caroline headed into the stacks. The little girl followed close on her heels.

Ten minutes later, Caroline's arms bulged with picture books and the surprisingly adult volume on aquatic life the child herself selected. Caroline marched toward the checkout station. Still, no sign of the librarian.

She bit back an inward sigh. "You'll have to wait—"

The little girl lugged Caroline toward a pint-size monitor. "Self-checkout. I do it every week after story time. I'll show you."

Caroline plopped the books onto the counter. The child scanned her card under a red-eyed laser beam. A beep sounded every time she ran the bar code on the back cover underneath the beam. A final printout scrolled out of the printer, and the child tore it free with a flourish. "This way you don't have to wait in line."

What line? The library appeared deserted. Not so different from Caroline's childhood. She had whiled away many pleasant hours here in the library while Lindi dated, Amelia went fishing and Honey played house. Caroline figured old Mrs. Beal had probably long since retired.

"Good." Caroline slung the strap of her purse over her shoulder. "Happy read—"

"Wait." The child caught her arm and halted Caroline's bid for freedom. "Maybe we could read one of the books before you leave."

Caroline pursed her lips. "Don't you have somewhere you have to be?"

The child shook her head.

A sense of panic mounted. Caroline wasn't good with children. "Won't your mother be looking for you?"

"My mother's dead."

"Oh…" Caroline's heart thudded. "So is mine," she whispered.

The child entwined her arm through the crook in Caroline's elbow. "Just for a minute." Her face scrunched. "Please…"

Caroline bit her lip. "The special word?"

The child nodded.

Caroline caved. "Okay…"

The child let out a whoop and then slapped a hand over her mouth. She giggled. Caroline giggled, too.

Finger against her lips, the little girl pulled her toward the sitting area near the entrance. And somehow Caroline found the both of them ensconced in a comfy leather armchair.

"My name's Izzie." The little girl extended her hand, adult-like. "For Isabelle."

Caroline shook her hand. "I'm Caroline."

The little girl curled into her side while Caroline read the short depictions and flipped the pages of a picture book about turtles.

Halfway through, Caroline glanced up to find twin pools of blue fixed on a tendril of Caroline's hair. Which had come loose from the practical chignon she'd wound on the nape of her neck for her early-morning aquarium meeting across the bay.

With a tentative touch, Izzie fingered the strand of Caroline's hair, a thoughtful expression on her small face. "I wish my hair was as pretty as yours."

At the child's plaintive words, Caroline laid the book across her slacks. Izzie's hair *was* a mess. Did her father never take the time to brush it?

"My hair was about the same auburn shade of

red as yours when I was your age. It darkened when I got older."

She feathered a springy coil behind Izzie's petal-shaped ear. "I always wanted beautiful, curly hair like yours. Mine is straighter than most sticks." And she poked Izzy in her belly with her index finger to demonstrate.

Caroline's breath hitched. Where had that come from? You didn't go around touching children. Especially children who didn't belong to you. Further proof she was no good with children.

But Izzie doubled over and laughed. "You're funny, Caroline."

Since when?

Lindi had been the pretty Duer girl. Amelia the tomboy and Honey the sweet one. Caroline had been known as the brainy sister.

Izzie flipped the book right side up. Her finger jabbed the page. "That's where you stopped. Finish…" She snuggled closer, practically in Caroline's lap. "Please…"

What parent left a child alone this long, even in a library? Somebody should've taught Izzie about stranger danger. According to the evening news, child abductions were on the rise. Not to mention serial killers.

Though unless things had dramatically changed since Caroline was a girl on the Delmarva Peninsula, those crimes rarely occurred on the isolated strip of land separating the Chesapeake Bay from the Atlantic Ocean.

But she couldn't deny a frisson of pleasure as the top of Izzie's red head scraped her chin. She inhaled the little girl scents of sea air, coconut oil and sunshine clinging to Izzie. Caroline propped the book so they could both see better.

Not such a bad way to spend a May morning. Anything to stall the coming confrontation she dreaded with her family. Put off the inevitable with her sisters and dad.

Because despite having returned to her Eastern Shore birthplace, Caroline feared she'd never truly be able to go home again. Not after what she'd done.

Weston Clark hunched over the blueprints spread over the table at the Sandpiper Café. His friend, and the former executive petty officer at the United States Coast Guard Station Kiptohanock, Sawyer Kole ran his finger across the etchings Weston had created in what would become Weston and Izzie's new home.

After buying the decommissioned lighthouse and keeper's station from the Coast Guard and after six months of remodeling, he—not to mention nine-year-old Izzie—was anxious to move into the new quarters. He'd promised Izzie one of the two rooms in the tower.

"Don't worry, Wes." Sawyer rested his fore-arms across the renderings. "It's going to be fabulous." He smiled. "With the ocean on one side. And the tidal marsh on the other."

Weston sighed. "It's a money pit is what it is."

Considering some lighthouses sold at public auction around the United States in the million-dollar range, he'd bought the property situated on a neck of Virginia land at a bargain price. This spit of land and the lightkeeper's station held special meaning for him.

His grandfather had been one of the last of the light-savers. History come full circle, preserving Izzie's heritage and finally establishing the home Izzie's mother had longed for. The home he'd been too self-absorbed and rootless in his upwardly mobile Coast Guard career to provide. Until too late.

Weston swallowed against the unexpected rush of feeling. It surprised him sometimes how grief engulfed him without warning like a rogue wave.

He checked his watch. Izzie would still be occupied at the Saturday story hour. He took a sip from his coffee mug. "How's Honey?"

Sawyer's arctic blue eyes lit at the mention of his bride of six months. Weston tamped down a prick of envy at his friend's happiness. A hard-won happiness the onetime foster kid truly deserved. Unlike Weston.

"Honey's good." Sawyer's lips curved as if he was reliving an especially sweet remembrance. "We're good."

An aching emptiness consumed him. At thirty-six, Weston believed that kind of joy had passed him by forever. Everything that happened between him and Jessica was his own fault.

Sawyer fiddled with the Shore-famous Long John doughnut on his plate. "I promise I'll finish the lighthouse remodeling well in advance of the foster kids camp."

"Everybody seaside knows you have the work ethic of ten men, but don't put so much pressure on yourself. Izz and I are making do in the light-keeper's quarters."

Weston warmed his hands around the mug. "A few months—give or take—won't matter. I understand Keller's Kids Camp needs to be your priority."

He'd been on a cutter during most of Jessica's pregnancy with Izzie. But he'd never allow Izzie to suffer again. Not because of him.

Weston cleared his throat. "Is the baby doing okay?"

Sawyer placed his arm across the back of the seat. "Honey swears the kid is practicing for the rodeo in utero."

The ex-cowboy Coastie had only recently completed his enlistment and returned to civilian life to oversee the kids camp where siblings separated by the foster system could reconnect for one week a year. Sawyer also helped his wife run the Duer Fisherman's Lodge.

"Any gender news to share? Or aren't you telling?"

Sawyer rolled his eyes. "Are you kidding me? Honey had to know. There was a nursery to decorate. Baby registries to fill out."

"Izzie got her invite to the baby shower last week. She's killing me wanting to go shopping." Weston grinned.

"Appreciate the warning." Sawyer laughed. "We're having a girl."

Weston reached across the booth and play-punched his friend's arm. "Way to go, Coastie."

"Ex-Coasties." But Sawyer smiled.

Wes glanced at his watch. The hands hadn't moved an inch. He tapped the watch face with his finger. Nothing. "Oh, no…" Panicked, he grabbed his cell off the table to check the time. Weston shoved out of the booth.

Sawyer rolled the blueprints. "What's wrong?"

Weston fumbled in his jeans for his wallet. "My watch stopped."

Sawyer motioned him toward the exit. "I got this today. Your turn next time. Another thing I've learned from my beautiful wife—never keep a lady waiting."

"Thanks. See you later."

With no time to stop and chat, Weston gave the ROMEOs in the adjacent booth a quick wave. The Retired Older Men Eating Out—grizzled Shore watermen and the volunteer Coastie auxiliaries—catcalled as he swung the glass-fronted door wide. The overhead bells clanged.

"Hot date, Commander?"

"Don't let us keep you."

"Give 'er a kiss from us."

He ignored them and charged across the village square toward the brick Victorian, which housed Kiptohanock's local library. His heart pounded. Izzie would be worried.

It was just Izzie and him. They counted on each other. They depended on each other. Each other was all they had. And he'd let her down.

Weston raced up the broad-planked steps of the library. Izzie wasn't a crier, but imagining twin rivulets flowing down her cheeks, he felt his gut clench. Frantic, he twisted open the brass knob on the stout oak door and dashed across the threshold inside. He froze at the sight that met his eyes.

His little girl snuggled in the arms of one of the most beautiful women he'd ever seen in his life. Head bent over a picture book, the woman softly read aloud to his daughter.

Weston took a moment to calm the staccato beating of his heart. To settle his fear. And to be honest, to enjoy the scene before him the way you would take pleasure in an exquisite painting.

The woman's elegant, long-sleeved white silk blouse was overdressed for the casual fishing hamlet. As were the navy trousers and sling-back pumps in a place where the preferred attire was flip-flops and shorts. A bun at the nape of her slim neck, tendrils of reddish brown hair framed the woman's oval face.

"Mahogany." With the woodworking he'd done of late, he should know. Her hair was the color of mahogany.

He hadn't realized he'd spoken aloud until the woman's gaze lifted.

Izzie scooted out of the armchair. "Daddy!"

The woman's eyes narrowed. Lustrous, chocolate eyes. He remembered the women at church talking about the new librarian Kiptohanock hired after old Mrs. Beal retired. But she was unlike any librarian he remembered from his boyhood days in Richmond.

The woman frowned. He'd been staring, mouth open. He closed his mouth with a snap and flushed.

Izzie flung herself at him, clasping him around the knees. He staggered and wrapped his arms around her torso as much to steady himself as to drag his eyes away from the new librarian.

"Where were you, Daddy? I've been waiting..."

The woman's lips tightened.

"I'm sorry, little lady." He kissed the top of Izzie's curly hair. "My watch stopped. I was at the Sandpiper going over the last of the remodeling plans, and I lost track of time."

The woman rose. Five foot sevenish to his six-foot height, he estimated. Folding her arms across her chest, she tapped one slim foot against the hardwood floor. Disapproval radiated from her set features.

"Izzie's father, I presume?"

Not a great first impression. He grimaced. Since when did he care about impressing a woman? Especially one so…so sophisticated. Because that had turned out so well for him before.

"She's been waiting a long time." The woman gestured at the now-deserted library. "All the other children went home with their mothers ages ago."

He winced. "As I said, I'm sorry."

The woman raised her chin. "Anything could've happened to the child. A father shouldn't be too busy to take care of his family."

Anger surged at the woman's arrogant assumptions. He bit off the harsh retort that rose to his lips. The desire to put the new librarian in her place.

Beautiful, maybe. Unfriendly, for sure. Strange, a woman like her would choose the public-pleas-ing profession of a librarian. 'Cause this woman had the social skills of a barracuda.

With his anything-but-stellar track record in the romance department, this was why he kept it just him and Izzie. Were all women as hard-hearted as Jessica? Or was it his misfortune to only run into those types?

"I'm sorry to have inconvenienced you..." He allowed his gaze to rake her face and the arm-chair full of books. A look he hadn't utilized since he commanded Coasties before Jessica's death prompted his abrupt career change. "Don't let us keep you from your shelving."

The woman's eyes enlarged. "I'm not—" An interesting blush stained her cheeks.

Izzie tried to climb up his legs. Bending, he scooped his daughter into his arms. She was getting heavy. Too big to hold.

But he'd hold Izzie close as long as he could. Because besides Izzie and a run-down lighthouse, what else did he have in his life?

Izzie captured his face between her small, warm palms and wrenched his attention from less pleasant thoughts. "She's Caroline. We had fun."

At her words, the woman—Caroline Who-ever—uncoiled a notch.

He reminded himself he'd been in the wrong. Not her job to babysit his child. He took a deep breath. "I apologize again. I'm doing the best I can."

That hadn't been enough for Jessica, though. And in Caroline's equally cool appraisal of him, he felt his every deficiency flayed bare.

His lips twisted. He'd never been enough for anyone.

Izzie squeezed her legs around his waist and hung her arms around his neck.

Except maybe Izzie.

Izzie lunged, and he almost dropped her. "My books, Daddy."

Caroline What's-Her-Name blinked. "Oh." She snagged hold of the seen-better-days library bag Izzie dragged along on every outing.

Weston took the bulging bag and sagged beneath its weight. "Leave any for the other children?"

His daughter giggled. "Daddy and I will see you next week, Caroline."

"I'm not…" Caroline's face did a fair imitation of Izzie sucking lemon rinds.

He gave the librarian a nice view of their backs. See her next week? He'd sit on the library porch while Izzie enjoyed story time if it meant avoiding another less-than-pleasant encounter with the stone-cold Caroline.

Who had the face of a Renaissance Madonna and the disposition of a killer shark.

Chapter Two

When she'd looked up from the pages of the book and found his smoldering blue eyes fixed upon her, Caroline's heart leaped in spite of herself.

Midthirties, she guessed. From his sweatshirt and his dark brown military buzz—close cut on the sides—probably an active duty or one-time Guardsman. A 'come here, not native-born to the Shore.

Through the library window, she watched the ruggedly handsome man tuck Izzie into the green Chevy Colorado parked beside the diner across the square. His broad shoulders under the gray Coast Guard Academy sweatshirt bunched as he leaned to fasten Izzie's seat belt.

Notwithstanding Caroline's fifteen-year absence from Accomack County, she didn't recognize him. She heaved a sigh. She didn't think she would've forgotten him had they previously met. Her gaze flicked toward the now-empty chair.

She'd enjoyed cuddling with Izzie. Who would've foreseen that? Not Caroline or anyone who knew her, she guessed.

Definitely not mother material. But no more stalling.

Caroline glanced at the mounted wall clock behind the librarian's desk. Guests typically left the Duer Lodge midmorning in pursuit of their day's activities.

She'd scheduled a lunch meeting with her longtime colleague at the Virginia Institute of Marine Science to finalize their grant-funded summer pilot program. If things went as well as she expected at the family homestead—which was to say, not well—she had someplace else to be.

Caroline turned her head toward the babble of voices at the top of the ornate staircase. Kiptohanock's real librarian emerged on the landing with a sixty-something matron Caroline—unfortunately—did recognize.

"Caroline Victoria Duer."

She squeezed her eyes shut. Escape so close and yet so far.

"Is that you? After all this time?"

A lot of water under that proverbial bridge, but some things—like some people—didn't change.

Including Mrs. Davenport, otherwise known as the Kiptohanock Grapevine.

Mrs. Davenport, plumper after fifteen years, descended the staircase like a bygone movie queen. "As I live and breathe, Seth Duer's second oldest come home at last."

Other Kiptohanock bookworms popped out from between the stacks across the hall to get a look. The twenty-something librarian's eyes blinked behind her fashionable horn-rimmed glasses.

Time, like sand in an hourglass, had run out for Caroline.

If she didn't beat the village blabbermouth to the punch, her father and sisters would learn of her arrival before she could get to the house. She couldn't hide any longer.

"Yes, indeed, Mrs. Davenport." She wrenched open the oak-paneled door. "The black sheep has come home at last."

Caroline drove around the square. Past the Sandpiper Café. The post office. The Coast Guard station. Recreational and commercial fishing vessels bobbed in the harbor. Fair-weather flags fluttered in the breeze. Beyond the inlet, barrier islands emptied into the vastness of the Atlantic.

The white clapboard church hugged the shoreline. Its steeple pierced the azure sky. Leafed-out trees canopied the side lanes, where the ginger-bread-trimmed Victorian homes fanned out from the center of the town square like spokes on a wheel.

Driving out of town, she averted her gaze from the cemetery on a high slope overlooking the marina. She'd finally found the courage to face her father and sisters. She didn't know if she had the courage to face the graves. Maybe she'd never have enough courage to face them.

Leaving the coastal village behind, she headed down Seaside Road, which connected the oceanside villages. Her heart pounding in her ears, she pulled off the secondary road into the Duer driveway. A simple sign at the turnoff read Duer Fisherman's Lodge.

Caroline stopped at the top of the driveway. Her hands white-knuckled the wheel. She paused to reorient herself with her childhood home. To prepare for the changes the devastating hurricane eight months ago had wrought. But on the surface, everything appeared the same.

She scanned the white, two-story Victorian with the wraparound porch. The picket fence still rimmed the shade-studded perimeter of the yard. The silvery surface of the tidal creek glimmered behind the house. She released her death grip on the wheel.

Home to seven generations of proud Duer watermen, including her father, Seth Duer, possibly the proudest of all. In the last century during the days of gilded grandeur, Northern steel magnates had "roughed" it at the Duer fishing lodge. Her ancestors had served as hunting guides in winter, oystered, crabbed and run charters in summer. But those days, like the steamers traveling the waters between New York City and Wachapreague, had long since passed.

She took a deep breath and released the brake. The car coasted toward the circle drive. The grand old lady, freshly painted and restored from the ravages of the storm, appeared better than ever under her youngest sister's watchful restoration. Caroline parked and switched off the engine.

Restoration... Her fondest hope.

She whispered a quick prayer and got out of the car as a tall, Nordic blond man in jeans and T-shirt stepped around the corner of the house from the direction of the old cabin. A phone shrilled inside. Then stopped.

He advanced, hand outstretched. "I didn't realize more guests were arriving today. I'm—"

"Sawyer Kole. Honey's husband."

He dropped his hand, confusion written across his craggy features. As if recognition teased on the fringes of his memory. The front door squeaked on its hinges.

Sawyer Kole's eyes went glacial at the same moment Honey gasped, "Caroline."

Caroline's gaze flitted to the honey-blonde woman poised on the porch steps. Whom she'd last beheld when Honey wasn't much bigger than Izzie. Now a lovely woman in her midtwenties and soon to be a mother. Caroline's eyes fell to her youngest sister's rounded abdomen. Caroline thought of little redheaded Izzie, and something stirred in her heart.

With great deliberation, Sawyer moved between them. Blocking Caroline's view of her sister. Protecting his wife. From her.

Voices drifted from the dock at the edge of the tidal creek. A carrot-haired boy, maybe Izzie's age, ran ahead. The strawberry-blonde woman, Caroline's younger sister Amelia, bounced a dark-haired baby on her hip as she strode up the incline from the water.

Catching sight of her, Seth Duer, their father, came to a dead stop. As fit as she remembered, though his hair beneath the Nandua Warriors ball cap and his thick mustache were more salt than pepper. His gray eyebrows bristled.

Oyster shells crunched beneath the little boy's sneakers. "Hey, Aunt Honey!" He waved. "Mimi, Granddad and I showed my baby how to bait a line."

The expression on her father's grizzled face froze Caroline to the marrow of her bones.

Amelia squeezed their father's elbow. "Daddy." The baby squirmed in her arms.

Seth and Marian Duer's third-born daughter. The tomboy son Seth had never had, but longed for. Renowned illustrator. Married to Braeden Scott, senior chief at Station Kiptohanock.

Amelia's face had shuttered with neither pleasure nor foreboding. Unable to get a read on her sister, Caroline glanced at the redheaded boy. Max. An old ache resurfaced.

Her older sister's boy. Born moments before Lindi died after a head-on collision with a drunk driver on Highway 13. Adopted and raised by Amelia, Max's beloved "Mimi." And Amelia was now also the mother of the toddler in her arms, Patrick Scott.

The silence roared between them until Max in his innocence broke it.

"Who's that, Mimi?" His eyes were so like Lindi's. "She looks like the other sister in the picture above the fireplace. The one you told me not to mention around Granddad."

Caroline flinched.

Seth's blue-green eyes, the color of Amelia's, too, flashed. "Don't worry about learning her name. She probably won't be around long enough for you to get used to using it."

Caroline and Honey had inherited their mother's dark brown eyes. Caroline frowned at the thought of her mother and pushed yet another memory out of her mind.

Amelia shifted the baby to a more comfortable position. "First, let's see why she's here."

"Please..." Caroline whispered.

Her father snorted. Then the tough, old codger scrubbed his face with a hand hard with calluses. "Come to rub our noses in her highfalutin jet-set lifestyle."

She lifted her chin. "You don't know anything about my life."

"Whose fault is that, girl?"

He'd yet to say her name, Caroline couldn't help noticing. As if he wanted no part of her. Her insides quivered. She wrapped her hand around the cuff of her left sleeve.

Seth crossed his arms over his plaid shirt. "There's two kinds of people born on the Shore, Max, my boy. Best you learn now how to identify them both."

Caroline gritted her teeth.

"Those who don't ever want to leave..."

She knew if she didn't get out of here in the next few minutes, she was going to implode into a million, trillion pieces.

"And those, like my runaway daughter." Seth

speared her with a look. "Who can't wait to leave and who never return."

"Until now, Dad. Caroline's come home." Always the peacemaker, her sister Honey. Far more than Caroline deserved from the baby sister she'd abandoned.

Caroline examined the set expressions on her family's faces. What had she expected? What else did she deserve?

"She never returned after her mother died," Seth growled. "Not for her sister's funeral. Not during Max's chemo. Not after the storm almost leveled our home." He clenched his fist against his jeans. "Not for a wedding. Or a birthday. Not even a postcard, much less a phone call."

And Caroline suddenly understood that nothing she could ever say would erase the damage she'd inflicted. Nor wash away the hurt of the past. This... This illadvised, ludicrous attempt at reconciliation was for naught. She spun on her heel.

"Don't go," Honey called.

"Let 'er go," Seth grunted. "Let 'er run away like before. It's what she does best."

"Daddy... Stop it," barked Amelia.

Caroline wrested the car door open and flung herself into the driver's seat. Whereas she'd found mercy and forgiveness in God, with her family there'd be none of either. She jerked the gear into Drive.

In a blur, she fishtailed onto Seaside Road. She pointed the car south and drove until the shaking of her hands wouldn't allow her to drive any farther. She pulled over on the other side of the Quinby bridge and parked.

Her shoulders ached with tension. Spots swam before her eyes. She leaned her head on the headrest, and struggled to draw a breath as her throat closed.

This had been a mistake. A terrible, perhaps unredeemable, mistake. She felt the waves of the darkness she'd spent years clawing her way out of encroaching. Like an inexorable tide, ever closer. A headache throbbed at her temples.

Her breathing came in short, rapid bursts. Hand on her chest, she laid her forehead across the steering wheel. Willing the anxiety to subside and the blackness to erode.

But the waves mounted and towered like a tsunami. Cresting, waiting to consume her whole. To drag her under for good this time into the riptide of blackness.

God. Oh, God. Oh, God.

Where was her purse? She fumbled for the tote bag in the passenger seat. The pills. It'd been so long since she'd relied on them.

She hadn't suffered an anxiety attack in several years. But with her so-called reunion facing her this morning, surely she'd had the foresight to tuck them inside her purse in case of an emergency.

Digging around through the detritus that filled her life, she came up empty. She slammed her hands on the wheel. Of all the days not to...

She breathed in through her mouth and exhaled through her nose in an exercise she'd learned from the counselor. And she repeated the Scriptures she'd memorized at the suggestion of a friend, a marine biologist working in the Bahamas.

Until the dizziness passed. Until her vision cleared. Until the pain in her lungs subsided.

Dripping with sweat, she took a few steadying breaths before shifting gears. Lesson learned. Despite the size of Kiptohanock, she'd avoid contact with her family.

One summer. The two-month pilot program. She'd lie low. Something she was good at.

And like Thomas Wolfe had said, you couldn't ever go home again. Or at least, not her.

"Daddy! Come quick! Daddy!"

Weston dropped the hammer and raced out of the former lightkeeper's cottage. He ran toward the beach, where the incoming tide lapped against the shoreline. Where he'd left his nine-year-old daughter alone… The librarian pegged him rightly. He was a terrible father.

"Isabelle!"

Panting, he plowed his way to the top of the dune. "Answer me." The fronds of sea oats danced—taunting him—in the afternoon breeze.

On the beach below, she windmilled her arms to get his attention. He willed his heart to return to a semblance of normal. She'd gotten his attention, all right. He scrambled down the dune toward his daughter.

She clutched the straw hat on her head. "Look, Daddy." With her free hand, she gestured to a set of tracks stippling the sand from the base of the dunes to where they disappeared around the neck of the beach. "Turtle tracks."

Izzie bounced in her flip-flops, a redheaded pogo stick. "Maybe turtle eggs on our beach, too." She clapped her hands together. The hat went flying.

He sighed, and watched it blow out to sea.

"We could have babies. Just like Max."

His gaze flickered to his daughter. "If there are eggs, they won't belong to us. Best thing we can do is leave them and their turtle mama alone."

Izzie's face fell.

He tickled her ribs. "Even Max will tell you to give new mamas a wide berth. They're touchy. And ornery."

"Was Mama touchy and ornery with me?"

"N-not when you were the most beautiful, wonderful baby who was ever born." He nuzzled her cheek with the stubble of his jaw.

"Daddy." She giggled and pushed his shoulder. "You are so prickly."

He caught Izzie in his arms and gave her a bear hug. "Like a porcupine."

Laughing, Izzie wriggled free. "I'm gonna follow the tracks to the water." She disappeared beyond the curve of the dune before he could formulate, much less express, a warning.

One day she wouldn't be so easily diverted from the rest of the story. And he could never tell Izzie the whole truth.

Behind the dune, Izzie screamed. He jolted, his heart palpitating once more.

"Daddy! Hurry…"

Parenting—not unlike certain Coastie jobs— ought to come with hazard pay. Breaking into a loping run, he jogged around the point.

He found Izzie at the edge of the surf, where the waves curled and skittered over her bare toes like a watery sand crab. She crouched beside a prehistoric-looking sea turtle. A metallic hook jutted from the creature's neck.

"Izzie, get back." He waved his arm. "Injured animals are dangerous."

"The turtle mama." Izzie sank to her knees. "She's hurt."

He came closer. The olive-gray carapace on the turtle's back was gouged and dented.

"She's just lying in the sand, Daddy." Izzie's eyes swam with tears. "I don't think she can make it back to her babies without our help."

How to explain this? "Turtles spend their lives in the ocean. Females only come ashore to lay eggs and then they leave."

Izzie glared at him. "They leave their babies?" Her voice rose. "Mamas aren't supposed to leave their babies."

"No, they aren't," he whispered. And he wondered what questions about her own mother he'd field later from Izzie.

"It's the turtle way, Izz." He ran his gaze over this relative to the dinosaur. "If this turtle didn't make it into the water by dawn, she's been baking in the sun for hours."

He lifted his ball cap, crimped the brim and settled it on his head again. "It doesn't look good for her, Izz."

"Please... Help her, Daddy." In her face, the unspoken belief her daddy could fix everything.

If only that were so.

He pulled Izzie to a safer distance as the turtle's flippers thrashed in the sand. He'd seen this before when he was stationed in Florida. One of the turtle's flippers was mangled, probably from a boat's propeller.

"We've got to save her, Daddy." Izzie tugged on his arm. "Save her so she can take care of her babies."

"Izzie." He squatted to his daughter's level. "Things like this happen. We have to let nature take its course. Mothers…" He gazed over the whitecaps. Izzie knew this better than anyone.

He cleared his throat and tried again. "Mothers die, Isabelle."

"No." Izzie jerked free. "You've got to do something, Daddy. Don't let her die, too."

His breath caught. Was that what his daughter believed? That he'd let her mother die?

But upon reflection of his many failures as a husband, perhaps he had. He stared at Izzie, this tiny replica of him and Jessica. And his heart hurt.

"No guarantees." But reaching a decision, he fished the cell out of his cargo shorts. "I'm an engineer, not a marine animal specialist, Izz. But I know where to find one."

"Thank you, Daddy."

How could he not try to save the turtle mother? Especially since it was his fault Izzie's mother died.

Chapter Three

"It's a critical time, Caroline. Peak season is approaching. I'm glad your team will be joining us seaside."

Caroline smiled at Dr. Roland Teague, a fellow marine scientist. They'd walked from the nearby Virginia Institute of Marine Science facility—VIMS—in Wachapreague to the Island House for a lunchtime meeting. Situated over the inlet on pylons, the bank of windows in the restaurant overlooked the tidal marsh.

She'd known Roland since her undergrad days at Virginia Tech. The fifty-something scientist had been a friend and professional mentor ever since. Clad in an outlandishly tropical shirt, Bermuda shorts and boat shoes, Roland hadn't changed much over the years. Except for the streaks of silver in his thinning Jimmy Buffet–style mane.

Catching her staring, Roland laughed. "What's gray, stays."

She laughed as he'd meant her to. "How's Danielle?" She owed Roland and his wife more than she could ever repay. They'd been a blessing in an otherwise very dark time in her life.

"Busy with the end-of-quarter classes at the community college. She said to tell you hello. She wants you to come over for dinner soon." Roland paused to take a deep swig of sweet tea. "I'm excited about this plan you've spearheaded with the aquarium board of directors in Virginia Beach."

After what had happened this morning with her father, she was no longer so sure that her personal involvement in the sea turtle project had been a good idea.

Roland set his glass on the tabletop with a dull ping. "Last year, we found sixteen nests on the Eastern Shore, though we're on the extreme northern limits of their nesting grounds. This year biologists are predicting record high numbers. We're overdue on the Shore for a rescue center of our own."

She swirled the batter-fried hush puppy in the small tub of butter. "Nesting is up along the entire coastline of the southeastern United States. We're not sure why. Maybe climate change and warmer weather has raised water temperatures."

"That's why your expertise is so invaluable to

us here. You've got an impressive résumé. Everything from the Caribbean and Central America to coordinating one of North Carolina's Outer Banks stranding teams."

An expert in aquaculture, he winked. "Not to mention you're a hometown girl and have an 'in' with the locals."

Caroline refrained from disabusing him of that notion. On her last research assignment in Virginia Beach, she'd pushed the idea of creating a rehabilitation center staffed by a few professionals and manned by interns in the high season to educate the local populace and serve as another Eastern Shore tourist draw.

She'd spent long hours with a planning committee formulating a cost-effective strategy. If the center was successful, she hoped the aquatic veterinary hospital would also eliminate the need to transport injured marine animals to treatment centers farther away. The animals most often did not survive transport. A hospital on the Eastern Shore would mean the difference between life and death.

"The center will bring much needed jobs on the Shore," Roland added.

She thought of her father and his stubborn refusal to accede gracefully to any change. "I hope Kiptohanock and the other coastal villages will catch our vision. If they decide to balk…" She bit off the end of the hush puppy.

"That's why the board sent you. You're our public relations secret weapon. With 'small-town girl makes good' as our leading advocate, what can go wrong?"

She traced the condensation on her tea glass with her finger. What could go wrong indeed? Without the backing of influential locals—like Seth Duer—the proposed center would die a quick death in the face of resistance to change and a deep-seated distrust of outsiders.

The Eastern Shore was isolated by nature. And the Eastern Shore population preferred it that way.

She grimaced. "No pressure there, Roland."

He popped a hush puppy into his mouth. He chewed and swallowed. "I have all the faith in the world in you, Caroline."

Glad somebody did. If she didn't believe so strongly in this program… If God hadn't clearly shown her it was time to go home and make amends, she'd… She'd be on a beach off the turquoise waters of St. Kitts.

"It's all hands on deck at this time of year. Sometimes we get ten calls a day from home owners, the Guard, game wardens and watermen."

She nodded. "Thanks for offering us access to

your laboratory here during the pilot program. My graduate students will arrive later today."

"They'll bunk in the dormitory with my summer interns." He speared a sea scallop with his fork. "I guess with family here, you'll be living with them and not on the economy as the Coasties say."

She was saved from making an embarrassing admission when Roland's cell, clamped to his belt, beeped.

"Teague here." His eyes widened. "Where?" He drummed his fingers on the tabletop. "I'll send her right away."

She tilted her head as he ended the call.

"You've got your first case." He grinned. "It was the marine animal hotline. There's a turtle stranded on a nearby beach."

"What species?"

He pocketed his phone. "Home owner didn't say. Probably wouldn't know a loggerhead from a leatherback anyway."

"Where did you say the turtle's beached?"

"Out on the Neck by the old lighthouse."

She scraped back her chair. "I haven't been out that far in years. Does the access road still connect the barrier island to the peninsula? Or was it washed out in the hurricane last year?"

"I'll text you the precise coordinates. But the

causeway is still intact. In great shape, actually, since a new owner bought the lighthouse from the Coast Guard. He's in the process of renovating the entire structure."

She rolled her eyes. "Another 'come here?"

He pushed his plate aside. "Speaking as a 'come here myself, don't sell us short too quickly. Go and do your thing. Saving the turtle plus winning the hearts and minds of our Shore neighbors."

She grabbed the bill. "Roger that." And gave him a mock salute. "I'm on my way."

Weston watched the gunmetal-gray RAV4 round the point. He finished cutting the board for the crown molding and dusted his hands across his cargo shorts. The SUV sped down the causeway to the neck of land upon which the lighthouse and keeper's cottage had been built over a hundred years ago.

Removing his work gloves, he cut his eyes at Izzie. She perched at the top of the dune, per his explicit instructions, awaiting the aquatic veterinarian the stranding hotline had promised to send.

The vehicle slid to a halt beside his Colorado. The door swung open, and a reddish brown head emerged from the car. Reddish brown...

He squinted, not believing his eyes. What was

the librarian doing here? Maybe she'd driven the vet out to their remote location. Weston scanned the RAV4 for other signs of life.

"Caroline!" Izzie clambered down the dune and flung herself at the librarian.

Who'd exchanged her business attire for rolled jeans and a Hawaiian motif T-shirt with the outline of a sea turtle and the word *Honu*. She'd threaded her lustrous hair through the back of a ball cap labeled Kiptohanock Marine Animal Rescue Center. Caroline looked as surprised as he felt.

He placed one hand on his hip. "You're not a librarian."

A smile lifted one corner of her full lips. "No." She hugged Izzie. "I'm not."

"You're a veterinarian?"

She disengaged Izzie's stranglehold around her waist. "You seem to be having a hard time wrapping your head around that. You don't think girls are smart enough to be vets?"

"Daddy says girls are smart enough to be anything they want to be. Smarter than boys more often than not."

"Oh, really?" Caroline quirked her eyebrow. "Good to know."

Her eyes flitted to the lightkeeper's cottage behind him and upward to where the lighthouse towered. "So you're the 'come here who bought this derelict relic of our Eastern Shore maritime history."

Weston crossed his arms over his chest. "Not so derelict anymore, thanks to hours of labor."

"Glad to see you're not one of those who come to play but never invest in the local economy."

He widened his stance, his feet even with his hips. A habit he'd never outgrown from his Coastie days. Born of keeping his balance on board the cutter amid surging seas. "We're here to stay. I've put in my own labor to make sure this place becomes our year-round home."

Izzie bounced on the balls of her feet. "Daddy and Sawyer are almost finished with my room."

"Sawyer?" Caroline's eyes sharpened. "Sawyer Kole?"

"You know him?"

She glanced away. "Not well." Her gaze returned to him. "And you'd be the former Coastie who bought this place. Commander Clark."

"It's Weston. I'm not in the Guard anymore."

His daughter grinned. "He's my full-time daddy now."

Those melted chocolate eyes of hers flicked to where his left hand rested at his side. And his heart did a quick jerk.

"Come on, Caroline." Izzie tugged at her arm.

"The turtle mama's hurt, and I think I've found her eggs."

The lady vet hung back. "Turtle mama?"

Izzie, unable to remain motionless, surged ahead.

He shrugged. "Maybe I've got a budding aquatic vet, too."

When she reached inside her vehicle, he noticed the five rows of beaded and metallic bracelets encircling one slim wrist. Caroline retrieved what resembled a tackle box. He tore his gaze away as the lady vet headed after Izzie.

He trudged through the sand beside her. "You work with turtles a lot?"

She plowed through the sand in her flip-flops. "I'm a turtle specialist, actually."

Full of nervous energy, Izzie came back for them. "Y'all are so slow… Come on, everybody."

He smiled. "Monkeys like you tire us old people out long before lunch."

The vet paused to catch her breath at the crest of the dune. She peered at the dark blob on the sand below. "Is that a—?"

She stumbled down the dune toward the beach. Izzie charged after her.

He shuffled his way toward them at a more sedate pace. "Is that a what?"

Placing the tackle box on the sand, Caroline

opened the lid and extracted a pair of latex gloves. "It's a Kemp's ridley."

"Is that good?"

Her forehead creased. "Kemp's ridleys are the most endangered sea turtles. The rarest of them all."

Izzie crowded closer to inspect what he surmised was the marine veterinarian's version of a doctor's black bag.

"Let her work, sweetheart. Give the turtle lady room."

Caroline gave him a curious look before she dropped to her knees.

He leaned forward. "I should've brought a beach towel so you wouldn't get sand on your clothes."

Above the briny sea air, the tantalizing whiff of the lady vet's exotic perfume allured his senses. Jasmine? he wondered, remembering one CG assignment on Oahu.

Caroline touched the torn right-front flipper. "No worries. Sand is an occupational hazard of my job." Her mouth tightened as she probed the depth of the hook protruding from the turtle's esophagus. "I'll need to transport the turtle for surgery."

"You've got to make her better." Izzie clasped her hands under her chin. "So she can take care of her babies."

Caroline rose and brushed the sand from the knees of her jeans. "You didn't uncover the eggs, did you?"

Izzie shook her head.

"Good." Caroline's gaze swept the beach and came to rest on the tire-like treads in the sand. "Most Kemp's ridleys are born on a narrow strip of beach in Rancho Nuevo, Mexico. Juveniles forage the eastern seaboard as far north as Massachusetts for food. They especially love the shallow waters of the Chesapeake."

Eyes on the tracks, she headed for the base of the dune. Izzie and Weston followed. When the tracks stopped, so did Caroline.

She pointed toward the disturbed area in the sand. "Most times the turtles camouflage the nest so well we can't find it unless we catch them in the middle of laying eggs. But our turtle—probably from her injuries—didn't do her usual thorough job. Lucky for us."

Izzie found Caroline's hand. "I'll take care of Turtle Mama's eggs till she can get better and come back."

Caroline frowned. "All seven of the sea turtle species lay their eggs on the beach where they themselves were hatched and then they head out to sea again. They don't stick around to make sure the eggs hatch, Izzie."

"But something could dig 'em up and eat the

babies. They could get lost after they hatch and never find their mama. We've got to protect 'em."

Caroline looked over Izzie's head at him.

Weston cleared his throat. "We need to let nature take its course. Not interfere, Izzie. They'll hatch or they won't, with or without us."

"No, Daddy." Izzie jutted her hip. "God put those turtle babies on our beach for us to help them."

"I'm going to need your help, Izzie, in lots of ways." She fingered the stack of bracelets on her wrist. "It's extremely rare for a Kemp's ridley to lay eggs anywhere other than Mexico. To my knowledge, this may only be the second case we've discovered. The first documented nest was found across the bay in 2008."

He caught the excitement in her voice. "So this is a big deal? We're making history."

Caroline smiled.

His stomach turned over as those melted chocolate eyes of hers melted him.

"It is a big deal. A very big deal."

Caroline squeezed Izzie's hand. "We're going to need to put stakes around the nest and markers. Because Kemp's ridleys are so endangered, it's important that we monitor the nest for the next few months of incubation to ensure that the hatchlings have the best chance of survival."

She moistened her lips. "I'm afraid I may wear out my welcome on your beach before it's over."

He broadened his shoulders. "You won't wear out your welcome with us, I promise."

"It's so exciting, isn't it?" Izzie threw her arms around Caroline's waist.

Caroline staggered, but hugged Izzie back. The turtle lady, he decided, was good with children. Or at least, with his child.

"I can't wait to tell Max."

Caroline's smile faltered. She let go of Izzie. "The fewer people trampling the beach, the better chance the eggs have for hatching. We'll need to erect a wire cage to fend off raccoons and foxes."

"By we, you mean me?"

The smile returned to her lips.

His breath stutter-stepped. It could become addictive bringing a smile to the turtle lady's face. He also decided maybe his initial impression of Caroline had been off base. Perhaps she was more bark than bite.

"If you wouldn't mind..."

Mind? He blinked. It took him a second to refocus. Oh, right. She was talking about the cage.

"What about me, Caroline? What can I do?"

She smoothed Izzie's hair. "I'll need your dad's help in loading the turtle into the kiddy pool in my car. But then it's going to take a gazillion gallons of water to fill the pool enough to transport the turtle. And that's where you come in."

Izzie quivered from her sand-encrusted toes to the top of her unruly red hair. "I can do that. I'm good at filling buckets. Will Turtle Mama be okay?"

Caroline made eye contact with his daughter. "I'm going to have to do surgery to remove the hook and repair her flipper, but there are no guarantees, Izz."

"Like in life," he interjected.

Caroline's lips thinned. "Exactly."

She moved her car as close as she could to the beach without damaging the fragile dune biosphere. With a great deal of effort—mostly his and Caroline's—they managed to shift the turtle from the beach and into the SUV. Izzie darted ahead of them and returned, looping them as they shouldered the hundred-pound turtle over the dune.

Teeth gritted, he muscled the primeval creature into the kiddy pool in the back of the vet's vehicle. "You do this on a regular basis by yourself?" he grunted.

"Usually the grad students help. Good thing Kemp's ridleys are the smaller sized among sea turtles or we couldn't have managed on our own."

After parking the SUV once again near the cottage, the lithe Caroline handed several empty plastic buckets to Izzie. "Would you be so kind as to fill these for me, Izz?"

He folded his arms across his T-shirt. "And you're welcome."

She tilted her head. "For what?"

He propped his hip against the open tailgate and nudged his chin at the turtle in the pool.

"Oh…" She shrugged. "I'm sure I would've somehow managed without you, but—"

"Is that your idea of a thank you?" He grinned. "Not really a people person, are you?"

She blushed a lovely shade of rose. "I'm better with animals. I spend most of my time with them. People are too…"

"Complicated?"

Her gaze shot to his. "More entangling than a fisherman's net."

Message sent and received. Like a warning shot fired across the bow. This woman wasn't looking for relationships.

Good thing he wasn't either. In his case, the burned child dreaded the fire. He found himself—against his better judgment—curious about what lay behind the beautiful vet's aversion to relationships, though.

Not any of my business.

Izzie hurried from the house. One bucket clasped in both hands, she sloshed water over the rim and onto her bare toes.

The turtle lady might not be his business, but Izzie was. He'd never seen Izzie attach herself to anyone like this female veterinarian. And frankly, the idea of Izzie forming an attachment to the prickly vet disturbed Weston.

On a profound level, to a degree, Weston wasn't sure he wanted to explore. He had Izzie's well-being to consider. It was her fragile heart he was thinking about.

Wasn't it?

Proud as if she'd single-handedly saved the free world, Izzie transferred the now half-empty bucket to the vet.

She smiled at his daughter. "Thank you, Izzie. You're such a big help."

Izzie took off at a run. "I'll bring the other bucket, Caroline," she called over her shoulder.

He straightened. "Let me—"

"I got it, Daddy. I'm not a baby." His daughter never broke her stride.

Caroline poured the contents over the turtle's carapace and into the pool.

"Will you take the turtle to the aquarium across the bay to Virginia Beach or up to Ocean City in Maryland?"

"Neither." Caroline gave the turtle's shell a small pat. "Fortunately for this injured lady, we're headed to the new aquatic rehab center I'm establishing in Wachapreague for the summer."

Izzie sloshed forward in time to hear Caroline's last remarks. "Yay! You'll be here the whole summer?" Bucket clutched at chest level, she bounced on her toes.

He and Caroline stepped back. But not soon enough. Water doused the tailgate and puddled at his and Caroline's feet.

Weston seized the bucket before further damage ensued. "Izzie… Be careful."

Izzie's lower lip quivered. "I'm sorry. I was trying to help."

"You are the best helper I've had in ages." Caroline placed her palm on Izzie's head for a millisecond before taking the bucket from him. "A little water never hurt anyone. Kind of refreshing in this early heat wave."

Izzie danced on the tips of her toes again. "So you'll be here the whole summer?"

Caroline concentrated on filling the kiddy pool. "Most of it."

Weston's stomach did a curious, roiling dive. A sliver of stupid anticipation coupled with a whole lot of fear. Not his business, he reminded himself.

"How's Turtle Mama?" Izzie scrambled onto the bed of the truck. The truck rocked. Caroline wobbled.

"Careful, Monkey Girl…" His hand cupped Caroline's elbow to steady her.

The lady vet's eyes cut from his hand to his face. He reddened and let go of her.

"I realize we haven't been formally introduced, but did you just call me a monkey?" Her lips curved into a smile. "Or should I assume that term of endearment was directed at Izzie?"

He decided the turtle lady had a nice smile. Nice sense of humor, too.

Weston's hand tingled from the touch of her skin on his. If this was his reaction to the less-than-sociable lady vet, he needed to get out more.

Izzie laughed. "Silly Daddy calls me his monkey all the time."

His Adam's apple bobbed. He nodded like an idiot. And flushed again.

Maybe the church ladies were right. Way past time for some female companionship. Nothing wrong with a friend from the opposite gender.

Izzie scooped a handful of water. "What's going to happen to Turtle Mama?" She allowed it to trickle through her fingers onto the turtle.

The turtle lady gave Izzie what he guessed to be a highly redacted version of the surgical procedure.

"Can I watch?"

"I'm afraid not." Caroline's brow puckered. "We try, like at the people hospital, to keep everything as sterile—I mean germ free—as possible. Have you ever visited a people hospital before?"

His daughter squeezed Caroline's fingers and hopped from the bed of the truck. "Last fall when Max's baby was born. Babies are so sweet." Izzie sighed.

Weston tweaked the end of Izzie's nose. "Babies are also smelly and loud and take your favorite toys."

"You know Max Scott?" Caroline's mouth pulled downward. "Of course you know the Duers, if you know Sawyer Kole. Everybody knows everybody in good ol' Kiptohanock."

Her lips twisted. "You can't flush a toilet at one end without the other end knowing."

Izzie snuggled under her father's arm. "Max and I are sorta friends."

Weston grabbed Izzie into a headlock. "Sort of doesn't quite capture it."

He ruffled Izzie's red mane. "Try *compadre* in mischief. Best buddy in mayhem. Bonnie to Max's Clyde. When they're not aggravating the tar out of each other, that is."

Izzie laughed and broke free.

Caroline reached toward Izzie's tousled hair. "You messed up her—" She dropped her hand. "Not my business."

No, it wasn't. Izzie's hair and his parenting style—which he was all too aware lacked a feminine touch—was none of the lady vet's business.

She shoved the turtle pool farther into the truck and slammed the tailgate with a bang.

Izzie plucked at Caroline's shirt. "But how will I know if Turtle Mama is okay?"

As if she couldn't help herself, Caroline brushed a stray ringlet out of Izzie's face. "I'll give you a call later and let you know how Turtle Mama—I mean the turtle—is doing. Okay?"

Her words were directed at Izzie, but she glanced at him. "I'll get your cell number from Roland."

"Roland?"

"Dr. Teague at VIMS."

Weston shifted. "I'm assuming you're a doctor, too."

She dropped her gaze and stared at her coral-painted toes. "I don't use the title much. Most people just call me Caroline."

Why did this feel like he was pulling line on a hammerhead shark? "Caroline… What?"

Her gaze skipped to the top of the lighthouse before returning to him. "It's Duer. Caroline Duer."

Weston rocked on his heels. "Seth Duer's absentee daughter?" His heart raced. "The daughter who abandoned her family for her career."

Could he pick 'em or what? He scowled. Yet another instance of epic misjudgment on his part.

Good thing he'd found out before it was too late. Too late for Izzie. And for him?

Tensing, he pulled Izzie closer and put distance between them and Caroline. The gesture wasn't lost on the intelligent lady vet.

She swallowed. "I see my reputation precedes me."

Then her face blanked like a hurricane shutter nailed over a window. "And yes. I'm *that* Caroline Duer."

Chapter Four

Recalling Weston Clark's fierce scowl, Caroline felt tears burning her eyelids the entire journey from the Neck to VIMS. Izzie tugged on heartstrings Caroline didn't know she possessed. And Caroline had been getting along so nicely with Izzie's handsome ex–Coast Guard father, too, until—

Until she told him her name.

"What can't be cured, must be endured." A saying of her father's, which had become a self-fulfilling prophecy for Caroline's life thus far.

At the sloshing sounds from the back of the SUV, Caroline monitored the Kemp's ridley from the rearview mirror. She sighed as she bypassed Kiptohanock for Wachapreague. She might not be able to bring about reconciliation with her family, but she could make a difference in the endangered turtle's life and with the other sea creatures she'd have a chance to save over the course of the summer.

She was pleased to find her interns moved into the dormitory when she arrived at the makeshift surgical center. She'd need their assistance to help Izzie's turtle mama.

Caroline bit her lip. In her experience, it was best not to get too attached to the animals. Much less attached to humans, who were unpredictable and unreliable. When and if the female was deemed sea-ready, the turtle would be tagged for tracking and released into the open ocean once more.

Hours later, Caroline emerged from surgery and wiped the sweat off her brow with her hand. Her students would settle the Kemp's ridley into the tank and monitor the turtle's vital signs.

She'd managed to save all but a small portion of one of the turtle's flippers. Barring infection, she was optimistic as to the turtle's chances of survival and eventual release into the turtle's natural habitat. Which, of course, was the ultimate goal of the pilot program.

Behind the westerly horizon of the trees, the setting sun cast a molten glow upon the water in the harbor. Still in scrubs, she paused on the steps of the institute to take in the view of an Eastern Shore sunset. Her stomach growled. Lunch at the Island House with Roland had been hours ago.

After she'd been on her feet for hours in surgery, dinner was her next priority. Perhaps she'd try the Sage Diner, a longtime Shore favorite, near the motel on Highway 13. It probably wouldn't be a problem getting a table, since the tourist season hadn't properly begun yet.

She was startled to find her sisters waiting for her in the institute parking lot.

Amelia gazed at her across the roof of the RAV4. "We need to talk, Caroline."

Caroline's bracelets jangled as her fist tightened around the key. "I think Daddy pretty much said everything there was to say."

Honey came around the car. "Daddy is like an old sea dog. His bark is worse than his bite."

"She's right." Amelia nodded. "Anger is easier for him to acknowledge than the hurt."

"Hurt I caused." Caroline gulped. "Anger I deserve."

"Daddy will move beyond both if you give him time." Honey touched her arm. "I'm sure of it."

Caroline shuffled her flip-flops in the gravel. "You're more confident of that than I am."

"I'm sure enough for both of us." Honey gave Caroline a small smile. "It's good to see you. I've missed you."

A lump the size of a boulder lodged in Caroline's throat. "I missed you, too, baby sis." She turned her face into the wind blowing off the water. "More than you'll ever know."

"We all missed you, Caroline."

Caroline angled at the pensive note in Amelia's voice.

"I hope you'll stick around long enough to work through this thing with Daddy. He's not been the same since you left."

Caroline chewed the inside of her mouth. "I'm sorry for hurting all of you. But when Mom died, I had to leave. I can't explain why—I don't expect you to understand—but I just had to go."

"I heard this afternoon about the pilot program. Everyone in Kiptohanock is speculating on where the permanent marine center will be located." Amelia joined them on the other side of the car. "It's a good thing you're doing. And if anybody can make it happen, it will be you."

Caroline sighed. "Thanks for the vote of confidence. Something else I don't deserve after abandoning the family."

Amelia caught hold of her hand. "Some of us know what you did, Caroline."

She stiffened. "You do?" A throbbing low in her skull began to ache.

Honey tilted her head. "When the hurricane last September nearly destroyed the inn and the loan to rebuild came through so quickly, Amelia, Braeden and I made inquiries at the bank."

Oh, that. Caroline willed her heart to settle.

"While others had to wait much longer for federal funds, we were able to begin rebuilding immediately." Amelia squeezed her hand. "It was you who put up the money. I don't know how you did it, but it was you who saved the house and put us back in business."

Honey's mouth quivered. "You saved my dream and something far more precious, time to rebuild my relationship with Sawyer so we could have our happily-ever-after."

Tears stung Caroline's eyes, but she shook her head. "You're making it more than it was. Money was the least—"

"Not the least," Amelia insisted. "Exactly what we needed when we needed it the most."

Caroline shrugged. "Everything except myself."

"You gave us what you could, which is why Amelia and I added your name to the title to the house."

Caroline shook her head. "I never meant for you to do that. I lost my right to call the house my home a long time ago. I only wanted to help, not lay claim to anything."

Honey's arm went around Caroline, fixing Caroline in place between her sisters. As if they were both determined she wouldn't run away again. Little did they realize, she was done running.

Staying and facing the fallout of her actions was part of her healing. Essential to becoming whole once more.

"It's a done deal. The Duer Fisherman's Lodge is as it should have always been—owned and operated by the family. Braeden, Amelia, Patrick and Max Scott. Sawyer, me..." Honey patted her rounded belly. "And Baby Kole. Seth and Caroline Duer."

Amelia jutted her jaw. "*We're* laying claim to *you*. The house belongs to you as much as any of us. And we insist you stay in the unoccupied cabin during your summer program."

"I already have a reservation at the motel in Onley."

Honey brushed her hair off her shoulder. "Dexter Willett and I go back to high school. We trade clients when one or the other's accommodations are full. So I called him and canceled your reservation."

Caroline crossed her arms. "You did what, Beatrice Elizabeth Duer?"

Honey laughed. "Not even Sawyer gets to call me that. And it's Kole now, Caroline Victoria Duer. Thanks in large part to you."

A smile tugged at the corner of Amelia's lips. "We're not taking no for an answer."

Caroline blew out a breath. "Daddy is not going to like it."

Honey wound a strand of hair around her index finger. "You let me handle Daddy. He'll come around." She fluttered her lashes. "I've had time in the years since we last met to work on that whole steel gardenia thing."

Caroline's lips twitched. "I'll just bet you have."

Back in the day, Lindi, Caroline and Amelia had often moaned about how Honey could wind their father around her infant pinkie. Not to mention the Honey Effect, as Mom once called it, upon the entire male population of baby sister's kindergarten class.

Caroline and Amelia exchanged amused looks. And for the first time, she felt a stirring of hope and the small beginnings of the sisterly camaraderie they'd shared. Until she threw everything away.

But enough with the regrets. The past was the past. Her sisters were offering her forgiveness and a way to move beyond the hurt.

"I'm sorry I missed your prom and graduations." Caroline rubbed one hand against the bracelets. "Your weddings and the babies, too."

"You're here now." Amelia grasped Caroline's chin between her thumb and forefinger. "You and Daddy need to make amends for both your sakes."

Her blue-green eyes, so like their father's, bored into Caroline. "And perhaps one day, when you've had time to get to know us again, you'll feel safe enough to trust us with the why of your leaving."

"I know I have a funny way of showing it, but I love you two," Caroline whispered. "My leaving was meant to save you from worse pain."

Honey wrapped her arms around Caroline. "That's almost exactly what Sawyer said to me once when I told him how you left without an explanation."

Amelia draped her arm across Caroline's shoulder. "I'm glad you're home."

For the first time in over a decade, instead of feeling trapped, Caroline felt rooted and restored.

Honey patted Caroline's arm. "I left Sawyer in charge of finishing dinner. That cowboy of mine has many wonderful qualities, but cooking isn't one of them. If you don't relish my corn pudding burned to a crisp, we'd best be heading home."

"Burning dinner won't improve dear Dad's disposition, either," Amelia noted.

"Whatever you say." Caroline adjusted the strap of her purse on her arm. "I guess I'm as ready as I'll ever be."

"I want to go see Caroline and Turtle Mama." Weston flipped the clam fritter in the frying pan. Maybe if he pretended to be busy, Izzie would let this whole thing with the beautiful aquatic vet go.

Perched on a kitchen stool in the lightkeeper's quarters, Izzie kicked the island with her sneakered foot. *Bam. Bam. Bam.* "Daddy?"

Bam. Bam. Bam.

"Fritters are almost ready, Izz. Can you set the table?"

Bam. Bam. Bam. He grimaced.

"Daddy…"

The dull thuds continued. Relentless as a jackhammer, she was going to drive him crazy. Which, he acknowledged, was probably the point in her dogged barrage on the wooden counter. To drive him crazy or make him take her to Wachapreague.

Bam. Bam. Bam.

He adjusted the heat on the gas range and wiped his hands on the dish towel slung across his shoulder. "Stop with the drumbeat. I told you Dr. Duer called and said the turtle came through surgery as well as could be expected. We'll check on the turtle's status again in the morning. It's time for dinner."

"Why can't we go see Turtle Mama after dinner?"

Izzie's pluck and hardheadedness would be assets in the workforce one day. He took a deep breath. Provided a deeply patient boss interpreted those qualities as persistence and initiative.

"We can't go because…" He also reminded himself he was the one with the Coast Guard Academy degree. Surely he could outwit a fourth grader.

She cocked her head at him.

"Because…" His rationale slipped like sand between his fingers.

He glanced out the window and inspiration struck. "Because we have to cordon off the nest of eggs."

"Oh, yeah. We're on guard duty tonight."

His heart sank. Not where he'd been headed with this. He'd had a long day and—

"But we can go check on Turtle Mama tomorrow morning before church, can't we, Daddy?" Those blueberry eyes of hers warred with his common sense.

"Dr. Duer probably has other patients, Izz. We don't want to get in her way."

"She said I'm the best helper she's had in a long time. I don't bother her." A tiny frown puckered Izzie's brow. "Do you think I'm a bother?"

Weston dropped his elbows on the counter and took her hands between his own. "No, Izzie. I think you're wonderful." He gave her a quick kiss on her forehead.

She giggled. "I love you, Daddy." She smiled

at him. Tiny lines radiated out from the corner of her eyes.

"I love you, too, Izz."

"So we can visit Turtle Mama tomorrow?"

Who could say no to that face? Not him, that was for sure. Not about something so obviously important to her as Turtle Mama.

His chest tightened. He hoped it was the turtle who was important to his daughter and not Dr. Caroline Duer. "I guess we can stop by."

Weston let go of his daughter's hands. "But I don't want you to get too attached to the turtle or the vet. When Turtle Mama gets better, she's going back to where she belongs."

"I know, Daddy." Izzie slid off the stool. "And the vet's name is Caroline." She busied herself setting out the napkins and silverware.

"The vet will only be here through the summer." Dr. Duer's earlier courtesy call had been abrupt, brief and impersonal.

He'd also made a few phone calls to a few of the older men in the CG Auxiliary who'd known the Duers and the prodigal Caroline for decades. "I don't want you getting your feelings hurt. She's a busy woman and by all accounts, not maternal—which means—"

"I know what maternal means." Izzie sniffed. "I think she'd make someone a nice mommy."

Eyes averted, she gave far more attention to

facing the knives in just the right direction than knives deserved. "I think Caroline would make me a nice mommy," she whispered.

Weston reared. "Where in the world did you get that idea? I'm not looking for—"

"Don't you think Caroline is pretty, Daddy?" Izzie cocked her head and studied him.

His thoughts about Caroline Duer shouldn't be said out loud. Not to his daughter. Like how the sight of Caroline Duer did funny things to him.

Nor how he'd found out the hard way beauty was only skin deep. That there were far more essential qualities to be prized.

"She likes me, Daddy. I can tell. I think if you'd be nice to her, she'd like you, too."

He stalled. "I do think she's very pretty," he conceded. "But it takes more than pretty to make a family." Or a mother.

Weston turned to the range to flip the fritters. "We don't have anything in common."

"You have me. You'd both have me."

He winced. If only that had been enough before. He'd never willingly put himself or his daughter through that kind of pain again. *Help me, God. What do I say to her?*

"Don't you want me to have a mommy again, Daddy?"

He closed his eyes and leaned against the sink.

"Don't you want to have a wife to love us again?"

What he'd not understood was how lonely his daughter was for a mother. He'd hoped and prayed he would be enough. His gut clenched. Yet again, he wasn't enough for anyone. How could he explain he was trying to save Izzie from further pain?

He swallowed against the bile rising in his throat. "I think a mommy and a wife would be a good thing, baby. Someday. But not Dr. Duer."

Izzie narrowed her eyes. "Who, then? And someday starts tomorrow, Daddy."

This daughter of his was way too smart to be nine. Way too smart to be his.

Had the time come for him to rouse himself from his comfortable cocoon and return to the dating world? He glanced at his daughter. If for nothing else, then for Izzie's sake. She deserved a mother's love.

Weston flopped the dish towel over Izzie's head. "Right you are. First thing after breakfast tomorrow, we'll head over to VIMS to check on Turtle Mama. And I'll see what I can do about getting a date."

"It'd be fun to go with someone to the Wachapreague Fireman's Carnival in a few weeks." Izzie dragged the towel off her head. Her hair—Caroline Duer was right about that at least—was a mess. "But not a date with Caroline?"

He shook his head. "Not with Caroline. We could never be more than friends, Monkey Girl."

And friends was stretching it. There were hidden depths to the aquatic vet. Jagged reefs submerged beneath her surface waiting to shipwreck the unwary. Caroline Duer wasn't safe. To neither his daughter's heart nor his.

"Daddy!" she yelled. "The fritters are on fire!"

Too late, he shut off the temperature gauge. He clanged a lid onto the frying pan and smothered the flames.

A silence filled the air. As did the acrid fumes of burned seafood. Izzie's stomach rumbled. He appreciated her not making a big deal out of his latest parenting fiasco.

She took the keys off the nail beside the door. "Fried chicken from the Exmore Diner, Daddy?"

He appreciated her not saying "again." No two ways about it. His Izzie was a trouper.

Weston took the dangling keys from her hand. "Sorry about this, Izz."

"No worries, Daddy." She smiled. "I like restaurant food."

Chapter Five

Dinner at the Lodge with the family was a fiasco, and not because the food had burned. Which it didn't, thanks to the combined efforts of Amelia's and Honey's husbands.

Her father didn't have much to say. Not to anyone, much less to Caroline. He shoveled the food into his mouth, murmured his thanks and barreled out of the house toward the dock claiming he needed to check the boat.

She jolted as the screen door off the kitchen slammed shut against the frame. Placing her napkin beside her plate, she half rose. "This was a mistake. I should go."

"No..."

"Please stay..."

At the simultaneous protest of her sisters, Caroline dropped back into the chair. The floorboards creaked overhead as the inn's lone guest settled in for the evening.

Braeden and Sawyer exchanged a look.

"Actually." Braeden, the dark-haired senior chief at Station Kiptohanock, wiped his mouth with his napkin. "Dinner went better than I expected. It's important to stay the course."

"I agree." Sawyer scraped his chair across the pine floor and stood. "The Duer sisters aren't the only stubborn members of this family." He reached for a serving platter to clear the table. "Apples don't fall far from trees for a reason."

Braeden laughed. "Ain't that the truth? Birds of a feather."

Honey cut her eyes at Amelia. "I think we've been insulted."

Amelia sniffed, but Caroline noted the sparkle in her eyes when she locked gazes with her husband. "I *know* we've been insulted."

Caroline's heart pinged. No one would ever look at her that way. She hugged her arms around herself. Which was only right, considering her past.

Max lined the peas on his plate in a row of military precision. "What does that stuff mean? Birds and apples?"

Braeden ruffled his son's carrot-top curls. "It means that people with similar character and interests tend to hang out together." He moved to help Sawyer clear the table.

Max crouched in his chair, his gaze at eye level with the edge of the plate. "No duh, Dad. 'Cause family sticks together. Is an idiom the same as an idiot?"

"In my case, Max…" Caroline handed Sawyer the empty bread basket. "It probably should be."

She held back a sigh and watched her married sisters perform what must be for them a well-oiled ritual. She regretted the time she'd missed with her family. She fought a stab of envy at the fine men each of her sisters had married.

Amelia collected the hot pads. "An idiom is an expression that says one thing but often means something different."

She frowned at her son. "Quit playing with your food, Max. Here's another idiom for you. It's time to either fish or cut bait."

Max turned his fork right side up and balanced the end over the rim of the plate. "What else is an idiom?"

Braeden flicked his eyes at Amelia. "How aboot stubborn as a mule?" The Alaska native flavored "about" with the typical *hoi toide*—high tide—lilt of Eastern Shore natives.

Amelia's lips curved. "How *about* it takes one to know one?"

Honey placed her hand over her stomach. "Don't look a gift horse in the mouth."

Sawyer grinned. "It takes two to tango."

Blushing, Honey swatted at him. He laughed and zigzagged out of reach.

Caroline disposed of the crumpled napkins in the kitchen waste bin. "Or from Dad's point of view, he'll be glad to see the back of me."

"Sounds like crazy talk to me," Max muttered.

Honey shot Caroline a triumphant look. "Exactly. Besides, you can't leave." She smoothed the maternity top over the basketball-size bulge of her belly. "The church ladies are giving me an early baby shower in June before tourist season begins, and I want you to be there."

"Oh, Honey. I didn't realize… Of course I'll be there." Caroline put her hand to her throat. "I'd love to be there."

Honey's face radiated a joy Caroline couldn't begin to fathom. "It's going to be the best summer ever with you home. All of us together again."

Not all of us, Caroline reflected. She'd deliberately avoided lingering in the living room, where the family portrait hung over the mantel. A photo taken on a long-ago summer day when Mom and Lindi were still alive. When Caroline had still been part of the family. Before the darkness had taken root and nearly destroyed her life.

Don't put your faith in me, she wanted to shout

as Honey headed toward the kitchen. *I'll let you down. No matter how hard I try, I always do.*

But she said none of those things. Instead, Caroline lifted the floral arrangement from the walnut sideboard and positioned it in the center of the table. Wildflowers. Queen Anne's lace. And those ubiquitous brown-eyed ditch daisies she'd noted Honey was so fond of.

"Thank you for agreeing to attend the shower." Sawyer edged alongside Caroline, his voice low. "It means everything to her."

Caroline bit her lip. *Please, please don't make me the object of her happiness. I can't be responsible for anyone's happiness. Not even my own.*

"One week, Sawyer." She held up her finger. "I'll give it one week, but if things aren't better between Dad and me, I'll spend the rest of the pilot program at the motel." She swallowed. "The tension wouldn't be good for Honey or the baby."

He nodded. "It's going to be okay. This reunion has been a long time in the making. And wrought by more prayer than you could possibly realize. I know for a fact Honey has prayed for your safe return every day since you left fifteen years ago."

Caroline's mouth trembled.

Max positioned a lone pea on the prongs of the fork. "Watch this, Aunt Caroline." He winked at her with a piratical gleam in his eye. His finger hovered over the end of his fork.

Amelia sauntered into the dining room. "Don't you even think about launching that pea like a cannonball."

He slumped in the chair. "A guy can't have any fun."

Braeden poked his head around the doorframe. "Why, I've got more fun waiting for you than you can possibly imagine, son. Helping me wash and dry the dishes."

Max groaned. And Patrick wailed from his playpen in the corner.

Amelia's head fell back. "This teething business is going to be the death of me."

"Patrick wants to help us, Dad," Max bellowed.

The baby placed his chubby fist in his mouth and continued to cry. Without conscious thought, Caroline found herself at the playpen as Patrick's arms reached for her.

She lifted him out, and Patrick laid his head against her shoulder. He sucked at his tiny fingers. She stroked the crown of his silky brown hair and hummed a tune her mother had sung when Honey was little.

At the sudden silence, Caroline pivoted with the baby in her arms. "Oh…" She blinked. "I'm sorry. I shouldn't have…"

She tried prying the baby off her chest, but he clung like a limpet to stone. "Here. He's your baby. You'd know best how to soothe him." Patrick grunted and hung on to her blue scrubs.

"You're doing fine without me." Amelia smiled. "I could use a break. And it looks like you've got the touch."

Her eyes widened. "What touch? You mean 'cause I'm a doctor? I'm an animal doctor, not a baby doctor."

"Mom's touch." Amelia's eyes welled. "You look so much like Mom standing there rocking him…" She took a breath. "You sound like Mom, too. It's like having her here again."

Caroline dropped her face into Patrick's soft curls. She inhaled the scent of his baby shampoo. Her heart pounded. She held her breath and waited for the encroaching shaft of darkness, but nothing came.

Perhaps she'd had it wrong. Perhaps the therapist had been correct. Remembering was healing. It was the denial which wasn't. Yet judging from her father's reaction to her presence, perhaps he, too, found the memories painful.

Something they had in common after all.

Caroline rested her hand on Max's tousled hair. "After you finish in the kitchen, maybe you and I could go out on the porch. I know a thing or two about science. We could build the catapult to beat all catapults if you'd like."

Max grinned. "Cool." He pivoted toward Amelia. "Can I, Mimi? Before bedtime?"

Amelia nodded. "For a little while, but it's a church day tomorrow. Bright and early." She faced Caroline. "I hope you'll join the family there."

Braeden held out his hand for Max. They departed to assist Honey and Sawyer prepping for tomorrow's guest breakfast.

Caroline hugged the baby. She'd hoped to avoid the Kiptohanock church. Last time she'd been there had been for her mother's funeral.

"I wanted to also apologize for not being there when Lindi d-died." Caroline steadied her wobbling tone. "I was the next oldest. It should've been me who took care of Max and Dad and Honey. Not you. You gave up art school for them."

Caroline tensed, expecting to find condemnation in Amelia's eyes. But only compassion rippled across her sister's features. Amelia feathered a stray curl behind her baby's tiny ear.

Patrick smiled at his mom, but lay content in Caroline's arms.

"Max is my son as surely as Patrick. God has a way of working things out." A smile played across Amelia's lips. "Sometimes in the giving up of what we think we need, along the way we discover what we want the most."

Caroline stared at her sister. "I love you, Amelia. And no matter however long Dad tolerates my presence, thank you for letting me come home."

"Looking back, you and Dad are so much alike. Including the way you suffer so quietly." She cupped her hand over Caroline's cheek. "We probably should've said or done something, tried harder…"

Caroline passed the sleeping baby to Amelia. "Not much anyone can do. We've each got to struggle through the tunnel of grief the best we can."

Struggle through till you reached the light at the end. Caroline wondered if that was what she was really doing, returning to Kiptohanock. And she also wondered if she'd ever manage to reach the light at all.

Amelia nestled her baby son in her arms. "Don't you give up." Her eyes flashed. "You hear me? Don't quit on us. And you'll make it. I know you're going to make it."

Caroline's heart skipped a beat. Somehow Amelia knew or suspected…

"So you'll come to church tomorrow?"

Might that be another step toward reaching the light?

She released a breath. "I'll try."

"That's as much as any of us can do. Just try."

"…baby shower next month…"

Facing Reverend Parks at the podium, Weston

heard the faint scrape of the hinges on the vestibule door. Beside him in the pew, Izzie started to turn, but he captured her shoulder with his hand and anchored her firmly in place.

"Eyes forward, Seaman," he whispered in her ear.

She made a face but focused on the stained glass depiction of Jesus in the garden of Gethsemane on the wall behind Reverend Parks and the baptistry. A focus that only lasted till the reverend's next remark.

"...know you church ladies will want to help celebrate this most momentous of occasions in Honey and Sawyer Kole's lives..."

Izzie tugged on his shirttail. "I'm a church lady."

He frowned and put a finger to his lips.

A welcome breeze from the unseasonably sultry early June morning wafted into the sanctuary, courtesy of the open door. Many of the older Shore buildings didn't have air-conditioning.

He inserted a finger between the collar of his polo shirt and his neck and tugged. Not a mistake he intended to make with the lighthouse renovation, ocean winds notwithstanding.

A lock of Izzie's hair fluttered. Turning, Izzie's face lit as if an internal light had switched on.

"Hey, Caroline." Izzie waved in a frenzy of motion. "Caroline's here, Daddy."

Across the sanctuary, blond, brunette, red and gray heads swiveled toward the foyer, where Caroline Duer stood frozen like a squid caught in bright lights. Then, like a boom on a sailboat, the townsfolk's gaze swung as one toward Weston and his daughter.

Izzie clambered onto the pew. Her knees pressed against the curve of the bench. "Sit with us, Caroline."

He took hold of his daughter. "Izzie," he hissed. "It's Caro—"

"Get down..." He peeled her off the pew.

Reverend Parks cleared his throat. "Great idea, Isabelle. Let's take a moment to greet each other on the Lord's day before we sing our first hymn."

He stepped off the platform and was the first to reach Caroline. Who was still paralyzed—apparently struck mute—in the middle of the aisle.

Weston grimaced, absorbing her embarrassment. If she'd hoped to slip in unnoticed, so much for that. Thanks to Isabelle Alice Clark.

As the congregation mixed and mingled amid the rousing piano rendition of "There's a Sweet, Sweet Spirit," Seth Duer remained immobile. His gnarled knuckles slowly turned white from clutching the pew in front of him.

Weston glanced over his shoulder. His pulse ratcheted as two rosy spots of color bloomed in the aquatic vet's cheeks. Caroline Duer needed a rescue. His throat constricted.

Izzie tugged on his shirttail. "Daddy, let's go say hi."

Before he could act, Max darted into the aisle and latched on to his aunt's hand. When he pulled her into the family pew, Seth Duer went ramrod stiff. Caroline lifted her chin and stared straight ahead.

The veterinarian appeared in that moment to Weston to resemble old paintings he'd seen of saints before the lions. And he found himself admiring her guts. She must have known coming home—coming here today—wouldn't be easy.

Owning the consequences of your actions never was. That he knew something about. His own hypocrisy smote Weston. He was ashamed of how he'd condemned Caroline yesterday at the lighthouse. He'd acted as judge and jury without knowing both sides of the story. And after what had happened with Izzie's mother, he was the least qualified person on the planet to be handing out judgment on anyone.

Weston's heart thumped with the longing to make things better for the veterinarian. To help her make things right with her family and the community. It seemed to him he'd never met a braver person. Not on a storm-tossed cutter. Nor a beleaguered sailor in the face of certain death. She was the most beautiful woman he'd ever seen.

Eyes narrowed, Reverend Parks called the assembly to order. Lips compressed, with great deliberation, he closed the flap of his e-tablet on which he kept his sermon outline. "Please take your seats."

Reverend Parks gripped the sides of the podium with both hands. "I've decided to change my sermon this morning to a passage dear to my heart."

Across the aisle, Weston couldn't keep his gaze from straying toward Caroline.

"Open your Bibles to the Gospel of Luke, chapter 15."

The reverend paused at the sound of flipping pages. Weston helped Izzie locate the Scripture in her petal-pink kids' Bible.

Reverend Parks waited until every eye met his. "Today…" His gaze roamed across the congregation before resting on Seth Duer in the third row. "I want to talk to you about prodigals."

Weston felt rather than saw Caroline flinch. Her chest rose and fell with the difficulty of taking a steady breath. His heartbeat accelerated.

Did the reverend intend to publicly humiliate Caroline Duer? He and Izzie hadn't been here that long. Not yet a year. Weston glanced around at the assembled congregation. The atmosphere was thick with tension. So silent you could have heard the fluttering of a butterfly's wings. His stomach muscles knotted.

He sensed that beneath the brittle exterior Caroline donned, there was an inner fragility. Which made her courage more remarkable. What did the reverend intend to say? Would his words destroy any chance the vet had for winning support for the marine animal rehab? Worse yet, would the next few minutes destroy Caroline herself?

Weston gritted his teeth. He unconsciously curled his hands into fists. He wouldn't allow them—Reverend Parks included—to bully the turtle lady. Not on his watch.

"'And while the son was yet a long way off,'" Reverend Parks read the Scripture, "'the father saw him and felt compassion for him. Ran and embraced him and kissed him.'"

Weston found himself holding his breath, praying for this unknown woman with whom his daughter had formed such an inexplicable bond. A bond he shared?

"And so we must celebrate." Reverend Parks leaned into the podium. "The child who was dead has now begun to live. A child who was lost but later found." Tears swam in his Delmarva-blue eyes. "A child who is very much like every one of us," he whispered.

What followed was a lesson in grace so tender and so profound those who were privileged to hear Reverend Parks that day would later declare it to be the finest exposition of the gospel they'd ever heard. Made more powerful by the usually soft-spoken man of God who spoke with such fire and passion.

At the last hymn, no eyes were dry. Reverend Parks made his way to his usual spot at the door to greet his flock. But as the last note died away and ascended into the wooden rafters of the old church, Caroline launched out of the pew like one of the rockets at Wallops Island. She lurched toward the vestibule, a stricken look on her face.

Izzie charged into the aisle before Weston could stop her. The reverend halted Caroline at the exit with a quiet word. By the time Weston caught up to them, Caroline had regained control of her breathing.

Reverend Parks took hold of her hand, "...my office... Tuesday morning...?"

Her eyes were hooded, but she nodded. Reverend Parks released Caroline's hand, and she hurried down the church steps to the lawn toward her car.

"I didn't get to talk to her, Daddy." Izzie's mouth quivered. "Not this morning at the rescue center, either."

He gnawed the inside of his cheek. Lost child returned to the Kiptohanock fold or not, he couldn't allow this woman to wound his child. Was avoidance the answer to wean Izzie from her attachment to the vet? Or would more intentional encounters disabuse Izzie of her affection for the complicated black sheep Duer?

Izzie pressed her cheek into the fabric of his shirt. His daughter was only now beginning to trust him with the things that mattered to her. And this woman mattered to Izzie.

"Come on." He captured Izzie's hand. "Dr. Duer?"

The lady vet rummaged in her purse for her key.

He hurried Izzie across the lawn. "Dr. Duer?"

The vet clicked a button on the key chain and reached for the door handle.

Weston towed Izzie into the parking lot. "Please wait… Caroline…"

Her head snapped up.

"You didn't say hello." Izzie flung herself at Caroline. "Why did you run away?"

Falling against the car, Caroline wrapped her arms around his daughter. "I needed some air. I…" She glanced at him, her face conflicted. "I'm sorry."

He wondered why she believed she had to apologize. After his cold condemnation of her yesterday at the lighthouse, he should be the one apologizing to Caroline Duer.

Weston's eyes were drawn to the pulse beating a furious tempo in the hollow of her throat above the neckline of her sleeveless sundress. "Are you okay?"

"I'll be fine." She looked away over the headstones on the adjacent hillside. "Eventually, I think..." She bit her lip. "Maybe..."

She laid her hand on Izzie's head. "Good morning, Ladybug. What's up with you today?"

"Daddy and I watched the turtle eggs last night to be sure nothing happened to them. We slept in a chair on the beach and did everything you said."

"A chair? On the beach? All night?" Caroline's eyebrow rose. "Kemp's ridley eggs have an incubation period of forty-five to fifty-eight days."

He gave Caroline a lopsided smile. "Izzie is nothing if not enthusiastic. Remind you of anyone?" He made a show of rubbing his back. "Thanks a lot, Doc."

She smiled back.

His heart did a curious flip. Someone should've warned him about Caroline Duer's smile. He'd gotten the impression she wasn't a woman given to smiling a lot.

She rocked Izzie in the folds of her dress. "I don't recall telling you to pull an all-nighter. It's early days still."

"We stopped by the lab before church, and one

of the college students said Turtle Mama was doing great."

Caroline cupped her palm over Izzie's cheek. "Yes, she's doing better than we expected." Her thumb caressed a stray freckle.

His heart lurched at her unconscious tenderness for his child. "Caroline—"

A beeping sounded from her purse.

"Oh. Sorry." Caroline released Izzie and scrabbled through her tote bag. She examined her cell phone. "A text from the intern manning the Stranding Response Team phone. We've got another incoming patient found by one of the Coastie fast boats."

She placed a quick kiss on Izzie's rumpled curls. "I'd better head to Wachapreague and meet them at the center."

"Wait, Caroline..." Izzie caught her arm mid-motion. Caroline's bracelets jangled. "I need to ask you a question first."

"Okay, Izzie." Caroline pulled free and fiddled with the stack of metallic and woven bracelets encircling her wrist. "What is it, Ladybug?"

"Are you going to Honey's baby shower?"

Caroline moved toward the car door. "Yes, I am."

Izzie inserted herself between the vet and the car. "Me, too. But would you go shopping with me and help me pick out something to wear?"

Caroline paused, her hand on the door. "Um…" She flicked her eyes at Weston.

"You have plenty of clothes you can wear, Izzie."

Izzie lifted her chin. "I don't have a dress." She gestured at the purple T-shirt and capris she'd worn to the church service. Every day in coastal Kiptohanock was casual. Sundays, too.

He folded his arms across his chest. "You don't need a dress to look nice."

"Caroline's wearing a dress. Doesn't she look nice in a dress, Daddy?"

His turn to stammer. "Uh…"

Actually, Caroline Duer looked like a well-groomed version of Jackie Onassis in flip-flops. Nice didn't begin to cover it.

Caroline tilted her head. And waited.

"Yes, she looks very nice, but that doesn't mean you…" He raked his hand over his head. "You know fashion isn't in my wheelhouse, Monkey Girl."

Izzie seized hold of the car door. "Caroline could take me shopping."

He reddened. "Izzie, I'm sure she's busy."

"I'd love to take Izzie shopping." Caroline gave him a defiant look. "Why don't you bring her to the rescue center later this week—say Thursday—about four o'clock?"

Izzie bounced on the balls of her feet. "Yay!"

"You don't need to—"

"And you're welcome." Caroline slipped behind the wheel.

His lips quirked. "Like you said yesterday, I'm sure I would've managed somehow, but…"

She laughed. "Not much of a people person, are you?"

He closed the door with a soft click. "People, like fashion, can be complicated. I'm better with blueprints."

Weston leaned his elbows against the car window. "Will you allow me to fix dinner after you and Izzie return from your shopping expedition? I could give you a tour of our home-slash-work-in-progress."

She smiled at him. "I'd like that. Till then?"

He nodded and pulled Izzie a safe distance away. Caroline waved as she headed out of the gravel lot.

Till then. His mouth went dry. Had he lost what little mind he still possessed? What had he done?

Chapter Six

Caroline didn't know what she found more disturbing. That she was having dinner with the Clarks. Or *how much* she was looking forward to having dinner with the Clarks.

Okay, with Weston in particular, although she was as equally thrilled to spend the afternoon with Izzie. Honey—the real Duer fashionista—had directed Caroline to check out a new boutique in Onancock.

The talk with Reverend Parks on Tuesday morning had gone well. He'd been surprisingly candid about his own struggles with grief after the death of his first wife and a child. He was easy to talk with and not shocked when she told him what she'd done three years ago. She couldn't believe she'd come clean to this near stranger. But she felt lighter after sharing her mistakes.

"I've known your father for years," Reverend

Parks told her. "My mother was the closest thing to a friend your grandmother Kate had in those days. My mother's greatest regret was in not acting sooner. In not forcing Kate's secret into the light of day and therefore preventing a tragedy."

Caroline shook her head. "I'm not sure I follow what you're saying."

"Hurts only grow more painful if not lanced before they fester." He'd dropped his gaze to his hands, steepled on his desk in the church office. "It was only after your father's heart attack that Seth finally opened up to me. Now we meet once a week over Long Johns at the Sandpiper. It's been good for both of us."

"Secrets? Grandmother Duer?" Caroline scanned the reverend's features. "I don't understand."

A frown puckered the bridge of the reverend's nose. "I thought..." He flushed. "I think you and your father should talk."

"Why can't you tell me?"

"Because it's not my secret to tell, and healing often comes in the telling. Would you like to meet again?" The reverend opened his hands. "Just to talk while you're here this summer?"

Caroline found herself agreeing. "Maybe over ice cream?"

The reverend patted his stomach. "Great idea."

She spent the next two days working with an IT student at the community college to create a website for the pilot program. She did a local radio interview and presented an informative turtle talk at the elementary school. Anything to keep from dwelling on what she'd gotten herself into—dinner with Weston Clark.

On Thursday, while waiting for Weston to drop off Izzie at the institute, Caroline fussed with a stray tendril of hair that refused to stay in place. This was such a mistake. What was she doing taking a child shopping? What was she doing accepting dinner invites from a man who made her heart beat in triple time?

This was insane. She ought to pick up her phone right now and—

"Don't you look nice?" From her office doorway, Roland's eyes twinkled. "No ponytail or turtle T-shirt today. Got a date, huh?"

She lifted her chin. "Absolutely not. I'm taking a little girl shopping."

Roland leaned against the doorframe. "That little girl wouldn't be Weston Clark's daughter, would it?" He laughed. "No wonder you ditched the jeans and flip-flops."

She pursed her lips and gave him a haughty look. "This is not because of Weston Clark."

Roland crossed his arms. "Don't overthink this, Caroline. Be open to the possibilities. Just enjoy yourself."

She focused on rolling her white shirtsleeves

over the cuffs of the brown cardigan. "I had a project meeting with the county commissioners this morning about a tract of land for the proposed rescue center." Adjusting her bracelets, Caroline sniffed. "There was no time to change afterward."

Roland cut his eyes out the window overlooking the VIMS parking lot. "Whatever you say, Dr. Duer." He smirked. "And I think your date is here."

"He's not my— Oh."

The little red-haired girl charged across the parking lot toward the entrance. Izzie's father, Caroline couldn't help noticing, wasn't moving so quickly. He probably already regretted asking her to dinner. Probably trying to devise a way to renege his offer.

"I'd say break a leg, but with those spiky brown heels you're wearing, you might anyway."

Grabbing her purse off the chair, she brushed past the grinning Roland and hurried down the hall toward the lobby.

Caroline didn't renege. When she made a promise, she kept it. But she also couldn't help sneaking a quick look at her makeup as she approached the glass-fronted door.

Izzie flung open the door. Arms outstretched, she barreled into Caroline and entwined her arms around Caroline's waist. Thrown off balance, Caroline rocked back a step to regain her equilibrium. Weston caught Caroline's elbow to steady them both.

When his hand touched her arm, her pulse jumpstarted. Tingles like ladybugs frolicking across her skin. And with the appreciative gleam in his eye, she was glad she'd taken extra pains with her clothes this morning.

Izzie yanked Caroline toward the exit. His hand fell away. And Caroline immediately missed its warmth on her arm.

"Bye, Daddy."

His brow creased. "Are you ditching your old dad so soon?"

Caroline teetered and put the brakes on Izzie's momentum. "I'm taking Izzie to Onancock to a new boutique. Don't worry about fixing dinner for me, but I promise I'll have her home by—"

"Are you dumping my dinner plans?"

She played with the swaying golden hoop on her earlobe. "More like letting you off the hook. I'm sure you've got more important things to do than—"

"Izzie and I have to eat, don't we?" he growled.

Why did Weston Clark take everything she said the wrong way? She was only thinking of him—and that was the understatement of the decade. All she'd done all day was think of him.

And her. Eating dinner. Together.

She'd spent the better part of four days trying to erase thoughts of him from her brain. In vain.

"You've got to eat, too." He scowled. "It's not a big deal."

She was making way more out of this than Weston intended.

Izzie pulled her toward the door. "Come on, Caroline... We're burning daylight."

Caroline's lips twitched.

His expression eased. "Stores close and sidewalks roll up around here come 6:00 p.m. in case you've forgotten."

"Roger that, Commander." She gave him a mock salute. "I'll have Seaman Clark home before then."

"And you'll stay for dinner?"

She gave him a sideways glance and twined that unruly strand of hair around her finger. "I'll stay."

A corner of his mouth lifted. "Good." He angled toward his daughter. "You've got the money I gave you?"

Izzie nodded.

He sighed. "Have a fun time, Monkey Girl. And you, too, Turtle Lady. Try not to buy out the store."

The turtle lady's lips curved. "Affirmative. You have yourself a good afternoon, too."

"Caroline..." Izzie tugged.

She allowed herself to be propelled out the door. And cast a swift look over her shoulder to Weston still standing at the entrance. A forlorn expression flittered across his countenance. As if he hadn't wanted to be left behind.

Her imagination, she decided. Time to himself for a single dad was probably a rare commodity. Like shopping with little girls was a rarity in Caroline's life. So she promised herself to enjoy this opportunity to the utmost.

On the road, she glanced in the rearview mirror to Izzie, buckled in the backseat. "I think any shopping expedition should begin with chocolate. How about we stop at Scoops and get a milk shake?"

Milk shakes, she had on good authority from Amelia, were less messy than cones.

The little girl's face shone. "I'm so happy I could bust, Caroline."

It had been a long time since her presence had made anyone happy. A numbed part of Caroline's heart unfurled. Like the apple-green leaves on the willow tree by the creek in spring after a dreadful winter.

"Me, too, Ladybug." She blinked away the moisture in her eyes. "Me, too."

Weston found himself listening to one of Izzie's CDs in the truck on the way home from

Wachapreague. Because without his chatterbox daughter, he couldn't stand the quiet. The afternoon yawned ahead of him. So with time heavy on his hands, on impulse he allowed himself to be sidetracked by the idea of a Long John and coffee at the Sandpiper.

He winced. That was the best he could do? First time in months with no Izzie, what a party animal he turned out to be. Did he know how to have a good time or what?

Maybe he should give the Kiptohanock single ladies a closer look. A short list, which despite the dinner invite wouldn't include Caroline Duer, no matter how fetching she appeared. Dinner was about Izzie's feelings. He, Weston James Clark, was immune to Caroline's charms.

Yeah, right. He grimaced at the remembered feeling of her hand in his. *But if it helps you sleep at night, keep telling yourself that, Weston, ol' buddy.*

Pulling into the parking lot between the Coast Guard station and the café, he waved to a Coastie crew departing on a fast boat from the adjacent CG dock. Only to be intercepted by Seth Duer exiting the diner.

"Uh, Weston…" Seth pulled at his bristly mustache. "Could I have a quick word with you?"

He nodded and followed the seasoned waterman to an empty booth. He'd heard tales of Seth

Duer's protectiveness of his daughters. Tales involving shotguns.

Small-town grapevines being what they were, Seth had probably heard about Weston's dinner plans. He'd set the old man's mind at ease. No shotguns needed in this situation.

A waitress, Dixie, extricated a pen from where she'd lodged it behind her ear. "Thought you'd gone, Seth Duer. You want seconds?"

Seth waved his hand. "I'm good." He focused his attention across the booth on Weston. "How *aboot* you?"

He didn't have a good feeling from the steely look in the waterman's blue-green eyes. "Just a coffee and Long John."

Seth pursed his lips. "This won't take long. Get it to go, if you like."

His gut sank further. Dixie arched her brow. "To go it is."

Dixie jotted something on her notepad and gave Weston's shoulder a commiserating pat on her way to the kitchen. An uncomfortable silence settled between the men.

Finally, Seth placed both hands, palms down, on the tabletop. "I like you, son. May I call you son?"

Weston gave him a curt nod.

"Fact is, I believe you to be a good, decent man."

He wasn't sure Jessica's father would've agreed

with Seth Duer's assessment of his character. After the way things had ended with Jessica, he wasn't sure he agreed with Seth Duer's assessment of his character, either.

"You're new around here. And that little girl of yours is a sweetheart." Seth's mouth thinned, and disappeared behind the mustache. "Despite Reverend Parks's words on Sunday, I can't in good conscience advise you to pursue any relationship with Caroline."

Weston's mouth fell open. "You're warning me off? For mine and Izzie's sake? Because—"

"Because family sticks together in times of need." Seth raised his chin, in a mannerism not unlike Caroline. "Family takes care of family, but Caroline only takes care of herself."

"I'm sure Caroline had her reasons—"

"You can't trust Caroline."

Immediate words of defense on Caroline's behalf rose to Weston's lips. But Seth was right about one thing. Weston was new around here. He didn't know why Caroline left her family so abruptly, never to return until now. Yet why would Caroline's own father say such things about her if they weren't true?

Every conflict had two sides to the story. He aimed to find out what would induce a woman like Caroline to abandon those who loved her.

And in doing so, perhaps find closure over the choices Jessica had made, too.

"Caroline's been kind to Izzie."

Seth snared him with a look. "And you're sitting here telling me there's no interest on your part in my daughter?"

Weston dropped his eyes.

"I'm not trying to be harsh, Weston. Only honest. 'Cause if you or Izzie are seeing Caroline as anything more than…"

He raised his gaze as Seth shrugged.

"She's not mother material. I don't want your little girl to get hurt the way…" Seth's eyes flashed. "Take it from me." Seth's mouth hardened. "She'll destroy your heart."

Just like Jessica.

But Weston feared Seth's warning for Izzie— if not him—might already have come too late.

Caroline couldn't remember the last time she'd felt this happy. Maybe since before her mother's cancer diagnosis and subsequent death. She glanced in the rearview mirror into the backseat, where, with shopping bags piled high, Izzie chatted nonstop.

Leaving Accomac, Caroline made a right turn onto the causeway spanning the tidal creek separating the Neck from the rest of the peninsula.

She darted a quick look at the car's dashboard. "In plenty of time for supper, Izz."

Izzie bobbed in the seat. "We'll give Daddy a fashion show of everything we bought."

She'd take her cue from Weston, Caroline decided. Cut dinner short if things got awkward.

Caroline barely managed to park beside the one-story white brick lightkeeper's cottage before Izzie unleashed the seat belt and swung the door open.

"We're home, Daddy!" Izzie yelled, and grabbed a shopping bag.

Caroline removed the key from the ignition. Home wasn't something Caroline could claim. And some of the afternoon's happiness dimmed for her.

She made her way around to the other side to collect the rest of their shopping extravaganza. She shouldn't have allowed Izzie to talk her into buying a dress for herself. But once inside the cottage, she'd separate their purchases and make a quick exit.

Then she spotted Weston. In a blue-and-white-plaid shirt with the sleeves rolled up, he stood, hands in his jeans pockets, on the cottage stoop. Again, a lonesome look on his face. Which brightened at the sight of Izzie hurtling across the crushed-clamshell path toward him. His gaze drifted to where Caroline waited by the car.

Her throat caught. He didn't look happy to see her. Not at all. In fact, he looked like he'd prefer anyone but her to be standing in his driveway.

"...Wait till you see what we bought... Caroline found shoes to match—"

"Shoes?" His eyes sharpened. "I didn't give you enough money for shoes."

Caroline moved forward. "It's okay."

His mouth tightened. "It's not okay. We don't take charity from anyone, much less... Go inside, Izzie."

"Daddy—"

Stricken, Caroline placed the bags at Izzie's feet. "Much less from a total stranger. Got it." She pivoted. "I apologize." She threw the last bit over her shoulder as she strode toward her car.

"Wait... Stay here, Izzie." The gravel crunched behind her. "I should be the one apologizing, Caroline. Please, don't leave. That came out harsher than I intended."

He hovered within arm's reach. "I'm sorry. It's been a..." He scrubbed a hand over his face. "A disconcerting afternoon, which dredged up personal stuff I believed I'd put to rest."

Weston took hold of her hand. "None of which is your fault. Please forgive me. I'm still getting the hang of not barking at civilians. Izzie will be disappointed if you don't stay for dinner."

A light breeze carried his scent to her nostrils. Old Spice, she thought. Masculine and clean. She studied him for a moment. Only the caw of seagulls and the crash of the waves beyond the dunes broke the silence.

Caroline lifted her chin. "Only Izzie?"

Those indigo eyes of his flickered. His mouth curved. "Izzie won't be the only one disappointed if you don't stay."

If she had a lick of sense, she'd get in her car and leave. This former Coast Guard commander obviously had problems of his own. She could barely cope with her issues, much less his accumulated baggage, too.

"We've got to show Daddy my dress, Caroline."

He gave Caroline a winsome smile. Her heart did a strange, palpitating dance. The corners of his eyes crinkled as if he sensed the attraction she felt for him. Did he feel the same way about her?

"Yeah, Caroline." The blue in his eyes deepened and beckoned. "What Izzie said."

So not fair playing the kid card. That and she liked the sound of her name on his lips.

Caroline lifted her chin. "You still owe me forty dollars for Izzie's shoes, Clark."

His jaw dropped. "Forty dollars? What are they made of? Gold?"

She shrugged. "Welcome to the preteen years, Dad. It only gets more expensive from here on out."

He groaned. "What have you done to my tough, little tomboy?"

Caroline laughed. "Izzie's still tough. But she'll also look fabulous the next time she bests Max."

He laced his fingers in hers. "Thank you. You're a very forgiving person."

Breathless, she realized he'd not let go of her hand.

She glanced toward the point where the setting sun streaked the water a molten gold. "A person who's been forgiven much should forgive much also."

He stared at her a minute. "Wise, forgiving and beautiful. All in one package."

She let her shoulders rise and fall. "Not really."

"Yes, really. But I get the feeling that like me, that wisdom has been earned the hard way."

At the understanding in his eyes, a long-dormant hope blossomed in her heart. A hope she'd buried since those terrible days after her mother passed.

"Daddy… Caroline… Are we going to eat or what?"

He threw his daughter a sheepish look. "Coming, Monkey Girl." He pulled Caroline toward the cottage. "We better get supper on the table before my inmate riots."

We? And he still had hold of her hand.

She was a scientist, after all. Trained to observe. What she observed was her heart ratcheted a notch at the feel of his hand in hers. And that scared Caroline.

Could she trust her emotions this time? Should she? Or would only more heartbreak result from allowing this man and child a place in her life?

Warm, welcoming light spilled out from the cottage, casting a path onto the ground. Izzie grabbed on to Caroline's free hand as if somehow she feared Caroline might bolt.

After a decade of feeling nothing but numbness, like a limb gone to sleep, she felt pinpricks needling her emotions as her heart came to life again.

Time to quit playing it safe? Time to move past the regrets. Toward the light of hope ahead?

Summoning her courage, Caroline crossed the threshold and stepped inside.

Chapter Seven

Weston watched as Izzie gave Caroline a personal tour of the lightkeeper's quarters. It didn't take long. First, the combo living and kitchen area. Then the two rooms at the rear of the cottage, which were their temporary bedrooms until Sawyer finished their new bedrooms in the attached lighthouse.

He busied himself boiling the water for pasta while Izzie introduced Caroline one by one to her collection of stuffed animals perched on top of the couch.

"They like spending the day here." Izzie gestured at the window. "Where they can watch the tide roll in and out."

At the counter, he diced strawberries for the salad.

Izzie patted the head of the furry monkey, her favorite. "I'll put them to bed with me later."

Loyal to a fault, though, she'd never admit in front of the other animals she had favorites.

She'd been two when he came home after a long cutter assignment to find Jessica missing and a friend's wife on Izzie duty.

He should've realized then what was going on. Weston tossed a handful of croutons into the salad bowl. He should've done a lot of things.

Growing up with two loving parents, he hadn't imagined there were women who wouldn't feel the same about their own offspring. It had taken him a long time—too long—to face what a mistake he'd made in marrying Jessica.

"They feel safer in bed with me when it gets dark," Izzie continued.

Caroline nodded. "Of course they do."

He stirred the pasta and stood watch. Caroline seemed intent, truly interested in what his child shared with her.

Izzie went from picture to picture hanging on the wall above the sofa. The Izzie Hall of Fame, he often joked.

"This is me when I was three at my birthday party. This is me when I started kindergarten." She smiled. "I was so cute then, wasn't I, Daddy?"

Caroline answered before he could. "You still are, Ladybug." She settled a quick kiss on the top of his daughter's head.

His heart thumped in his chest. Despite what Seth Duer said, despite what Caroline said about herself, she was very, very good with his child.

Izzie slipped her arm around Caroline's waist. "This is me when I lost my first tooth..."

For a moment, his eyes blurred. His motherless daughter was soaking up Caroline's attention and affection like the sand soaked in the rays of the sun. Uncomfortable with the emotions, he angled himself toward the oven to check the bread.

"Doesn't look like hot dogs. It's spaghetti night."

He straightened to find Izzie perched on the stool, her elbows planted on the counter. Caroline eased into the adjacent chair. "What an astute observation." He tweaked Izzie's nose.

Izzie fluttered her lashes at him. "It had to be spaghetti or hot dogs."

Caroline placed her chin in her cupped hand. "Why's that?"

"Daddy's not a good cook."

He opened his mouth to defend himself, but Izzie beat him to the punch. "Spaghetti. Hot dogs. Or we go out." Izzie made a show of exasperation. "We eat out a lot. And I mean a lot..."

"Hey." He threw the dish towel slung over his shoulder at Izzie.

Izzie grinned and batted it away.

Caroline laughed. "It smells delicious. Are you sure I can't help you do something?"

"Daddy needs all the help he can get."

He started around the island and growled. Shrieking, Izzie jumped off the stool. She ducked behind Caroline's chair. "Save me, Turtle Lady."

Caroline's eyes sparkled. "With my life, Ladybug."

He shook his head. "Didn't you say something about a fashion show before dinner, Miss Food Critic?"

Izzie giggled and danced out of his reach. "I'll be right back," she promised, and hurried away.

When Weston returned to the small kitchen, he found Caroline stirring the hamburger browning in the skillet. "It was about to burn."

He sighed. "Thanks. I get distracted."

"I can see why." Caroline smiled and his knees almost buckled. "Izzie's a wonderful distraction."

She wasn't the only one.

Caroline gathered the plates and napkins. "I'll set the table for you."

He tried for a nonchalance he didn't feel. Not with her so close and comfortable in his home. As if she belonged. As if she'd always belonged here with him and Izzie.

And he suddenly knew that no matter what anyone else said, no matter the leftover fears he carried from Jessica—what he wanted most right now was to get to know this beautiful and intelligent woman.

Not just for Izzie's sake, but for himself, too.

Caroline couldn't stop a surge of pride when Izzie emerged in the dress and shoes they'd picked out together.

Izzie flung her arms wide. "Ta-da!"

Caroline's gaze cut to Weston. A mixture of emotions flitted across his face.

"Aren't I beautiful, Daddy?"

He came out from behind the kitchen island. "The most beautiful nine-year-old girl I've ever seen."

Izzie smoothed the ivory linen dress with the black lace princess collar and grinned. "Do I remind you of my mama?"

He flinched.

At the awkward beat of silence, Izzie touched a tentative hand to the silk headband they'd found to accessorize the outfit. "Daddy?" Her voice quivered, uncertain.

Blue fire blazed from his eyes with an emotion Caroline couldn't define. Raw pain. And anger?

Caroline rose from the stool, her hand outstretched as if to somehow protect Izzie. From what, she wasn't sure. Weston Clark would no more harm his daughter than she would. Yet something she'd glimpsed in his gaze—in his memories?—she suddenly feared might harm Izzie. "Weston…"

He jerked and seemed to come back to the man she knew—barely knew, she admitted. A man devoted to his child. A man—she swallowed—she very much wanted to get to know better.

Weston took Izzie's hand. "A Kiptohanock princess." He twirled her under his arm.

Izzie laughed, and Caroline relaxed.

"A princess with her own tower," Caroline teased. "A lighthouse tower I can't wait to see."

"Dinner's almost ready." He gave Izzie a brief hug. "Better change, Izz. Wouldn't want you to get sauce on your pretty party dress." He nudged her toward the hallway.

"Aye-aye, Captain." Izzie went into regulation stance and saluted him. "Wait till you see the dress we found for Caroline. It looks just like mine." She pivoted on her heel and headed for her bedroom. "We match."

Caroline bit her lip.

He cocked his head. "Match? Like in mother and daughter dresses?"

"I'm sorry, Weston. I didn't think about how it would…" She slumped. "I should've never let her talk me into buying it. Only I didn't bring a fancy dress with me across the Bay Bridge and—"

"And Izzie wanted you two to match so much."

"I'm sorry."

He returned to the kitchen. "You said that already."

She hated that she could no longer gauge his expression. "I'll return the dress first thing tomorrow."

Weston plated the food. "And disappoint Izzie?"

Her head started to pound. She cut her eyes to where she'd stashed her purse and the pills. If worse came to worst...

Who was she kidding? Worse had already come to worst one time too many times in Caroline's life. And now she'd made an unforgivable blunder with this man and the child she cared so much about.

She fluttered her hand, a motion he failed to see with his back to her. "I'll get a replacement. It'll be fine."

"I'm well aware of how persuasive Izzie can be." He faced her, plate in hand. "A replacement? Is that how you see yourself?"

She flushed. "I was only trying to be her friend. I'd never try to replace Izzie's mother."

And then the strangest expression of all crossed Weston's face before his eyes shuttered. "Maybe you should," he murmured as if to himself. "You'd be far better than the nothing she's had so far."

Caroline's eyes widened. She wasn't sure she'd heard him correctly.

"I'm baaack…" Izzie floated into the room in her usual T-shirt and jeans.

Weston smiled. "Yes, you are and just in time for dinner."

He pushed a plate at Caroline through the cutout separating the kitchen from the eating area. "Let's eat, shall we?"

Dinner was both less and more than Caroline expected. Less tension—none, in fact. More fun. More comfortable than she'd allowed herself to imagine. Small talk wasn't a problem with Izzie around.

Caroline found herself sharing memories of a childhood on the Shore. Happy memories of sun-drenched summers, crisp autumn skies, the beauty of the fog-shrouded tidal marsh in winter. And her vision for a marine rescue center.

The food was good. The conversation and company even better. In the glow of the hurricane lamp on the table, a portion of the loneliness she'd carried with her for so long seeped away.

Izzie managed to drag out of Caroline the moment she decided to become a turtle lady. It had begun with a turtle entangled in one of her father's nets in the old days before stricter fishing regulations were put in place.

"Dad and I carefully cut away the rope and lowered the turtle over the side of the *Now I Sea*. I was so proud because Dad said he needed my help. We watched the turtle—a loggerback, I realize now—slip beneath the blue-green waters of the inlet and disappear from sight." Caroline leaned against the back of her chair.

Weston took a sip of sweet tea. "So it was your dad and that experience that inspired you to become an aquatic veterinarian."

"I love my dad…" Izzie squeezed Weston's hand.

The gesture caught at Caroline's emotions, the ones she tried so hard to keep in check. "I love my dad, too. I just wish—" She blinked and looked away.

"Were you close?"

She gave him a sad smile. "When he could drag me away from the hurt animals I collected. He's always loved animals, too. Something we shared. Amelia was his fishing buddy. Lindi and Honey were Mom's little shadows."

Caroline sighed. "It wasn't always easy finding a place for myself in the family." She blew a breath between her lips. "Or now for that matter."

"Beneath the hurt and anger, he loves you, too."

"We don't always get do-overs, though."

His eyes became hooded. "No, we don't." He scooted back his chair. "So we need to make the most of today. Izzie, let's show Caroline the lighthouse."

"The dishes." Caroline rose. "Let me—"

"Dishes can wait." He stacked their plates and left them on the counter. "Come on. Wait till you see what we've done."

Izzie yanked open the wooden door in the wall Caroline had spied earlier. "Come on, you slow-pokes."

"We're keeping it closed off until the construction phase is over and the dust settles." He ushered her through.

Caroline's breath hitched.

He grimaced. "Bear in mind, it's a work in progress."

She touched his sleeve. "It's wonderful."

Caroline surveyed the unplastered redbrick walls in the circular-shaped room. The exterior door probably led directly to the beach below. A curving staircase spiraled upward. Not unlike the chambered nautilus shell on the mantel above a restored hearth.

"My grandfather's. It was the only thing he brought with him when the Coast Guard closed this place in the 1950s. He kept it mounted on a shelf in his study in Richmond. Reminded him of home. Like you, he grew up here. From a long line of lightkeepers."

Izzie dangled over the baluster railing at an angle that made Caroline dizzy. Proving Monkey Girl was an apt nickname. "Daddy says that's our family's special gift—we shine the light."

He shrugged. "She makes it sound far more noble than—"

"In an increasingly dark world—" Caroline lifted her chin "—I'm not sure there's a more noble legacy to have than that."

"This will be the new family room, and the cottage will be renovated once we move into our new quarters upstairs." A light sparked in his eyes, which she'd not seen before. "The kitchen area will be enlarged, and the cottage bedrooms will become my office."

"Amelia said you were an engineer."

He gave her a lazy grin. "You've been talking about me with your sister?"

She fiddled with the long gold chain dangling at the front of her brown cardigan. "Don't flatter yourself. No more than idle curiosity, I assure you."

He laughed.

Caroline's lips curved. "Though in looking at the progress you've made in such a short time, I'm guessing there's nothing idle about you. When do you find time to run your company?"

His face lost some of its humor. "I've put that on hold for a few months. My partner's running things in my absence. I'll be able to work from home once we complete the remodeling on the cottage, probably by Labor Day."

Weston moved toward the stairs, where Izzie,

ever impatient, had already disappeared. "Let me show you the rest."

Topic changed. A touchy subject, his work sabbatical. Best left alone. Caroline would remember that next time. Her cheeks burned as she followed him up the staircase at a more sedate pace. Assuming there was going to be a next time.

Izzie's room was everything Caroline believed a princess in the tower's room should be. But there, Weston called a halt to the tour.

"You've got school tomorrow, Monkey Girl."

Izzie groaned. "It's only eight o'clock…"

With a start, Caroline examined her wristwatch. The time had flown. Must be the company.

He herded Izzie downstairs to the cottage. She smiled as Izzie scooped up her stuffed animal menagerie. Yes, definitely the company.

"I'll be right back." A pucker formed between his brows. "Promise you won't go anywhere. Okay?"

Her heart accelerated. "I won't," she whispered.

"Good." He tapped the doorframe before disappearing into the hallway. A valve squeaked, followed by the sound of running water.

She occupied herself with washing the dishes. She'd set the kitchen and dining area to rights when Weston reappeared. He'd taken time to comb his hair. The aroma of fresh soap with hints of Old Spice emanated from a man who already rocked her senses. The Old Spice reminded her of her father.

"I didn't mean for you to do the dishes."

"My pleasure after the wonderful dinner you prepared."

Weston stroked the beard shadow on his jawline. "According to Izzie, one of the two dishes in my entire culinary repertoire."

"A great dad who's in no way defined by his cooking prowess."

His mouth pulled downward. "As in lack thereof. And I wasn't always a great dad." He frowned. "I was a terrible father, but I'm learning and trying to make up for what happened before."

"You don't have to explain anything to me."

"I want to." He twined his hand through her fingers. "And no one is more surprised by that than me."

She stared at their locked hands.

"Also, I want to show you the rest of the lighthouse. Including the gallery, where Izzie isn't allowed to go by herself. The view will take your breath."

Looking into his eyes, Caroline decided the view wasn't so bad from where she stood. But she allowed him to lead her toward the lighthouse tower.

Past the cozy, future living room. Up the stairs.

Past the landing where Izzie's room was located. Upward they climbed. Caroline paused to catch her breath on the top landing.

She peered over the banister. "Now I know how you keep in shape." She could've bitten off her tongue. "I mean..."

He made a show of flexing his biceps. "Glad to see you noticed."

She made a show of rolling her eyes and motioned toward the black-hinged door on the landing. "What's in there?" Her turn to change the subject.

He threw open the door. "The master bedroom."

She stepped across the threshold as he fumbled for the light switch, revealing circular walls painted a *cielo* blue, and a mahogany floor minus furnishings.

"It takes minimalist to a whole new level." She strolled over to one of the tall windows encircling the room and gazed below at the rhythmic pounding of the surf on the beach. "Literally."

He shuffled his feet on the polished floor. "Honey put together Izzie's room. I haven't decided how I want my room decorated, so I've left it bare for now. More important projects to work on first. I'll throw in some furniture eventually and call it done."

She did a slow three-sixty. "The sea views

alone… Above everything with only the sound of the wind… In daylight with the sunshine pouring into these gorgeous windows—"

Weston propped against the wall with an interesting smile on his face. "My thoughts exactly. Sawyer and Honey think I'm crazy to roost here in this eagle's aerie of a room."

He scratched his head and gave Caroline a slow, steady smile. "'Course most folks think I'm crazy in the first place for rehabbing a derelict lighthouse into a home."

Weston waited for Caroline's reaction. And she didn't disappoint.

She lifted her chin. A gesture he was finding increasingly endearing. "I know a little something about crazy. Trust me, this isn't even close."

"And then there's all those stairs…"

Her lips quirked. "Well, there is that. They may have a point."

"Speaking of stairs, think you can handle one more flight to the lantern room?"

"Lead the way, Commander Clark."

He found it increasingly impossible not to smile in this woman's presence. She'd have him grinning like a buffoon all the time if he didn't watch himself. "Ex-Commander."

At the top of the stairs, he leveraged open one

final door with his shoulder. He gave Caroline an apologetic look. "A work in progress, remember?"

She smiled. And he couldn't help himself. He smiled back. Caroline Duer—aka Turtle Lady—lightened his life in ways he hadn't experienced since…

He stepped out of the doorway to allow Caroline through. Since never.

"The light…" Like steel to magnet, she headed toward the enormous light in the center of the glass-studded room. "I didn't think the Coast Guard used these anymore."

She ran her fingertip over one of the multifaceted prisms.

"The Coast Guard doesn't. When they automated most lighthouses in the 1950s, this one was decommissioned. Now with cheaper light stations anchored and floating in troublesome channels, the new systems don't require the manpower this type of lens demanded."

"Does the lens still work?" The awed hush to her voice filled something empty in his soul. Her delight pleased him in a way he hadn't expected.

"Not yet. But I'm working on it with Coast Guard officials. For rare, ceremonial occasions."

"Your most amazing project ever."

He shook his head. "Izzie is my most important project. The lighthouse is merely a boyhood dream come true. Icing on the cake." He pulled her toward a glass door in the wall of glass. "There's more I want to show you."

She favored him with a sweet smile. And his heart sped up. He drew her out onto the gallery.

The wind buffeted them. She wrapped her cardigan around her body. He stepped closer to block the wind. "I should've brought my jacket."

"It's fine. You were right. This is glorious."

He gestured toward the string of lights to the south. "Kiptohanock." And to the north, "Maryland."

With one arm keeping her sweater in place, with her other hand she tucked a strand of hair the wind had unloosed from the bun at the nape of her neck.

He gave in to the urge to touch the mahogany tendril blowing across his cheek. "Not much for hairdos, I'm afraid."

She stilled at his touch, but she didn't step away. He feathered her hair behind her ear. The vein in the hollow of her throat thrummed with a beat as steady as the pull of the tide.

Weston felt himself drawn by the tug on his heartstrings. But beyond the attraction, he sensed dark, turbulent waters inside this woman. A riptide that could possibly leave him far out to sea.

He refused to ask her why she'd left her home and family. He wanted her to trust him enough to share the details of her past with him. Despite the danger shouting in his head, he wanted to share the deep places in his own life with her.

Weston took her in his arms. She didn't resist. He lifted her chin with the tips of his forefinger and thumb. A look of fear, disbelief and hope shone in her eyes. The pulse at the base of her throat beat furiously now, matching the drumming of his heart.

She leaned closer. He tilted his head. Her lips parted and he felt her breath on his cheek. He held his breath.

Then she pulled back. "I can't," she whispered. "I'm too much of a mess. My family…" Her eyes darted to the sky studded with stars like diamonds on blue velvet.

He let go of her. "I'm scared, too. I'm a mess, too." Weston wanted to kick himself. Too fast, too soon for whatever secrets Caroline battled.

She backed as far as the railing allowed. "You don't know what I did."

"Nor what I did, either."

Her brown eyes flicked to his with uncertainty.

Exposed to the elements, he wondered if he dared to come clean—if he cared enough to try and bridge the gulf between them. Would his willingness to share his dark places help her overcome her own? Or would Caroline lose all respect for him?

Chapter Eight

"I met Izzie's mother after I graduated from the academy."

Out on the gallery, Caroline glanced over a few feet to where Weston gripped the railing.

"Looking back, I see now how young and unsure of myself I was on my first duty assignment. She needed me so much. It bolstered my flagging confidence."

He faced Caroline. "But no excuses. I was raised to know better. Jessica got pregnant, and we got married." His gaze rested on Caroline as he waited for her reaction.

"You're not the only young person to make poor choices. But you tried to make things right as best you could." She touched his hand, cold on the iron railing. "As any honorable man would."

"Not so honorable. Marriage was the only way I could convince Jessica to keep the baby. She wanted to—" He took a ragged breath. "But as the pregnancy progressed, Jessica came more and more unglued. Hormones, I rationalized. Uncontrollable bouts of crying bordering on hysteria. The clinginess and dependency mushroomed."

A sinking dread formed a knot in the pit of Caroline's stomach.

Weston raked a hand over his head. "Her all-consuming need scared me. And then there were the unpredictable fits of rage."

He stared far out over the ocean waves. "When I got the chance to go to sea, I'm ashamed to say, I jumped at the opportunity to get away from her for a few weeks. She went into early labor." He closed his eyes. "I left her to have Izzie alone."

Caroline pressed her shoulder into his. "Early labor, you said. Doesn't sound like you intentionally abandoned her to go through that by herself."

"I've always wondered if while I was gone, Jessica did something to make herself..." He swallowed. "To get me back in port."

"And after Izzie was born, did things get better?"

"Worse." He clenched his jaw. "Postpartum depression, the doc said. I didn't know how to help Jessica. She wouldn't get out of bed for days on end. She begged me to leave the Coast Guard. To stay home with her. To make a home for her."

His mouth tightened. "Instead I poured myself into my career."

"Your safe place."

He frowned. "How did you know?"

Clutching the railing, she turned away toward the choppy sea.

He sighed. "I forced Jessica to see a doctor. The pills helped." He grimaced. "For a while, at least."

"They always do." Caroline's lips twisted. "For a while."

"I rose quickly through the ranks. Cutter duty became my respite from real life. I was ashamed of how I'd failed Jessica and the baby. I hid the truth from my crew and commanding officer."

Caroline threaded her arm through his. "You can't blame yourself for everything."

He shook his head. "I realize now, every time I left port Jessica found other options to satisfy her emptiness."

Caroline squeezed her eyes shut.

"Only Jessica's out-of-control behavior wasn't the big secret I believed." He pounded the railing with his fist. "While I was away, she spent her evenings clubbing and her days sleeping it off. I didn't know any of this until one of the other officers' wives stopped by the house one day and found Izzie alone and crying in her crib."

His voice broke. "She hadn't been fed or changed in who knows how long. Jessica was gone."

Caroline leaned her forehead against the solid bulk of his arm. "Wes…"

"The other wives rallied, God bless them. The station chaplain and his wife, too. I was helped off the cutter. Those first few weeks…" He exhaled. "My mom and sister flew in from Richmond, or I'm not sure how Izzie and I would've survived."

"And Jessica?"

"She'd met a rich executive. He promised to fulfill her biggest dreams. So she ditched us." He laughed, the sound without mirth. "Truth be told, I deserved to be ditched. But Izzie? That's something I've never understood."

Caroline sighed. "She wasn't in her right mind, Wes. She wasn't thinking."

"Oh, she was thinking, all right. About herself. She didn't have to leave Izzie alone. She could've called my mom or Social Services. That's what I've struggled with the most—forgiving Jessica for that."

His voice quivered. "And forgiving myself for ever putting Izzie in that dangerous position because of my pride. Anything could've happened to her, Caroline. Anything."

"Izzie doesn't know about her mother, does she?"

His chest heaved. "Would you tell a child something like that? About the person who's supposed to love you the most?"

She hugged him.

"Those days were the darkest of my life. Jessica cited me in the divorce papers for abandonment." His face shadowed. "And she was right. I'd abandoned her emotionally long before she left us."

"I know about dark days, Weston."

He pulled her closer. "I somehow thought you might. But despite everything—no, *because* of that—that's when I came back to the God of my childhood."

Weston rested his chin on the top of her head. "If perhaps I'd come to Him earlier... If I'd been the man, husband and father I should've been, then Jessica might have found in Him what she so desperately craved in me."

Caroline pulled back far enough to catch his gaze. "None of us can be that kind of enough for somebody else, Wes. I, too, learned that the hard way. The would-haves, could-haves, should-haves will kill you, trust me."

"The never-dids killed Jessica. Despite her new life with the big house and new husband, only the booze and narcotics helped her feel better, albeit temporarily. Intoxicated, she plowed her Corvette into a tree five months after the divorce."

"Only a strong man could've managed to survive everything you've been through and become the wonderful father you are to Izzie."

He favored her with a small smile. "Only a man with a strong faith in God."

"Thank you for trusting me with what happened, Wes."

"Maybe when Izzie's older, I'll tell her the truth. After the both of us have had years of living the life God meant for us."

"And God led you here."

He blew out a breath, releasing, Caroline prayed, more pieces of the pain. "Full circle to my family's lightkeeper legacy."

"Pretty cool."

Weston touched her nose with the tip of his finger. "You're pretty cool for understanding the heavy stuff I just laid on you and still wanting to be my friend." He cocked his head. "You still do want to be my friend, don't you?" His eyes searched her features. "Or perhaps more?"

Caroline's heart raced. Hope surged. But fear rose in her gut, clenching her insides. Quenching the light.

She tore her gaze away. "I'm only here for a few months." She was surprised at how steady her voice sounded. "Best not to complicate either of our already complicated lives. Friends would be good, though."

"Friends." He didn't sound pleased. "If that's what you want."

She stepped away. "That's what I need."

"For now."

Weston Clark wasn't a man used to failing to find a solution to every problem. Jessica had been his most spectacular failure. A failure he didn't intend to repeat. Wes was lonely. Caroline was lonely, too.

But he'd only find in her an equally frustrating, unsolvable dilemma. Perhaps her real purpose in returning to the Shore this summer might not just be reconciliation or building a marine rescue center.

Perhaps she might offer a transition, a bridge to healing for Weston and Izzie. From the pain of the past to the bright hope of tomorrow. Discovering a future with a woman who could be the wife and mother they both needed.

Sadness engulfed Caroline. Not her, but the sort of good woman a man like Weston deserved.

"Want to know what I've learned from rehabbing this old lighthouse?" His voice broke through her bleak reverie. "One of many lessons, but maybe the best lesson of all."

She raised her chin. "What would that be?"

"This place proves none of us need to be defined by our past forever."

He gazed over the railing. "From here, the past and all those problems recede to their rightful perspective. 'Cause up here we can see the problems the way God sees them. From His all-en-compassing view."

She peered at her RAV4 and Weston's Chevy parked below the tower. At the base of the dunes, neon tape fluttered in the ocean breeze and cordoned off the precious nest of turtle eggs.

"This place reminds me that with God's help I can redefine myself and forge a new future if I've the courage to try."

Exactly why Caroline had returned home in the first place. She pressed the bracelets against her flesh.

His eyes pinned her. "Do you have the courage to try, Caroline? To see what the summer holds?"

Oh, how she liked the way he looked at her. She gulped. "I'm leaving as soon as those eggs hatch."

Weston pursed his lips. "Consider me warned. Dinner tomorrow night? You can try out my other culinary achievement."

"Hot dogs?" She laughed. "With an enticing offer like that, how could I refuse?"

Weston's eyebrow arched. "How indeed?"

She poked him in the chest. "Persistent, aren't you?"

"One part persistence plus one part perseverance has gotten me this far, haven't they?"

The same could be said of her, as well. She and Weston had more in common than he knew.

More than what a good man like Weston ought to have to endure twice in one lifetime.

To Weston's chagrin, Caroline canceled on him for dinner. In her defense, Braeden recruited her for a rescue mission involving an injured dolphin, hit by a recreational boat operator near one of the barrier islands.

Another week flew by with the last week of school activities, which he diligently attended as a classroom dad. The only classroom dad in a sea of moms whose unabashed friendliness made him feel like a rooster at a hen party.

He and Sawyer labored long into each night on the lighthouse. Trying to get as much done before school let out for summer and Izzie roamed underfoot. The first round of foster siblings for Keller's Kids Camp were also inbound on Monday.

From brief texts and snatches of phone calls, a hectic week for the fund-raising turtle lady, too. Thanks, in part, to him. He used his Coast Guard Auxiliary contacts to put Caroline on the docket as keynote speaker to plead her case for the rescue center at the group's monthly breakfast meeting.

Because he believed in the worthiness of her cause? Of course. But it also gave him an excuse to see her. When he showed up to the church fellowship hall to offer his support, a smile tugged the corners of her mouth as they shared a long look across the crowded room.

"You did good." He grinned at her later across the toy display at a nearby baby store. "We make a convincing team. I think their support will clinch the funding you need."

"Is that why I let you convince me to drive to Onley to shop for a baby shower gift?" In a classy violet blouse and pleated linen skirt, she cocked her head. "Remind me why I'm doing this? I hate shopping."

He sorted through the stand of baby bibs, rompers and blankets. "'Cause you missed me?"

She smirked. "Try again."

He threw a stuffed gray elephant at her. "Hey."

She caught it in a one-handed swipe. She cut her eyes around the boutique. "You're going to get us kicked out of the only baby store this side of Salisbury." She returned the elephant to the shelf.

"Good reflexes for a turtle lady." He held up a crocheted pair of pink baby booties and inspected the price tag. "Seriously?" He placed the booties back on the shelf. "How about 'cause friends don't let friends shop alone?"

She seized hold of the booties. "They're precious, Wes. So cute…"

"I think you're cute."

She gave him a sidelong look and put the booties down again.

"Actually, that's wrong. I don't think you're cute."

She gave him her full attention then.

He smiled. "I think you're beautiful."

Two spots of color reddened her cheeks. She folded and refolded a fuzzy pink chenille blanket. But a smile softened the corners of her mouth.

"Besides, neither you nor Izzie has purchased a gift for this all-important social event of the Kiptohanock season."

She rolled her eyes. "You mean, the otherwise nonexistent Kiptohanock social season."

"Do you hate it here so much?"

"Surprisingly, no. I love getting to know my nephews and spending time with my sisters. I'm always happy if I can be close to the sea, too."

"And your father? Is it still awkward?"

Her eyes dropped. She flipped through the book *Goodnight Moon*. To stall or to compose herself, he guessed.

"Awkward would be an understatement. We stay out of each other's way for the most part, which is the only reason I've remained at the cabin. He's busy with fishing charters, and I'm spending most of my time at the rescue center."

"But that isn't close to the reconciliation you'd hoped for."

She shrugged. "Hope is a commodity I've learned not to indulge in. Too costly in the long run."

It gutted him to realize how something—or someone—had wounded Caroline so deeply. In some ways, she was still as entangled in the snares of her past as the marine life she rescued.

Weston longed to cradle her in the circle of his arms. But he dared not. "I don't know how you—how anyone—survives without hope, Caroline."

Her lips trembled before she regained control. "Listen to you, getting all serious on a shopping expedition." She threw a fluffy sea horse at him.

It bounced off his chest and fell to the carpet. He feigned a look of mock outrage. "Are you trying to get us kicked out of the only baby store between here and Salisbury, Turtle Lady?"

Her lips twitched. "My apologies."

Weston lifted a frilly pink dress for her to inspect. "What about this?"

She clasped her hands under her chin. "Oh, Wes. It's perfect. It screams, 'Honey's baby girl.'"

He broadened his shoulders. "Stick with me, Turtle Lady. I may only have two meals in my culinary wheelhouse, but I'm a guy with hidden talents."

Weston snatched the sea horse off the floor. "This would be a perfect gift for Baby Kole from you. Combining the undersea world of Aunt Caroline with Daddy Sawyer's cowboy inclinations."

She tapped her index finger on her chin. "You're good. You're very good, Commander Clark."

"That's what all my women say." He leaned over the display. "My mom and Izzie."

She laughed. "Modesty must be another one of your hidden talents."

"Why, thank you, Dr. Duer."

"Very well hidden talents."

The urge to grin overwhelmed him again. He needed to play it cool. He'd learned his lesson the other night. Caroline Duer spooked easy. "I'm assuming you'd like the store clerk to wrap these for us."

Caroline, still smiling, examined a child-sized bucket and spade. "You'd be assuming correctly. Wrapping is more Honey's forte. I don't wrap presents; I stitch wounds." She shoved two sets of binoculars in the bucket.

"Who's that for?"

"Presents for everyone." She hefted the bucket to shoulder height. "This is for Patrick and the binoculars are for big brother Max."

"You've got two binoculars in there."

"Something for Izzie, too. She and Max will have a blast checking out the wildlife."

"Izzie and Max will have a blast spying on the neighbors," he protested. "And you don't have to give Izzie anything."

He touched Caroline's cheek with his finger.

He waited for her to pull out of his reach, and was rewarded when she didn't. "Your time and attention are the only gift Izzie wants. You mean the world to her."

She winced. "Don't say that, Weston."

He berated himself for again saying the wrong thing. Pushing her. "Don't shut us out, Caroline. Don't shut me out or yourself from the possibilities of what-if."

"There's plenty of obstacles still ahead for the marine center. Including the Watermen's Association endorsement." She grimaced. "Which means Seth Duer."

"You don't have to do this alone, Caroline. Reverend Parks is a powerful ally in the community." Time to dial it back a notch. "Not to mention yours truly."

He pretended to shine his knuckle on his shirt. "Not that I like to brag."

She shook her head. "Brag? You?"

"You and I make a convincing team…"

She snagged the pink booties. "I like these. My treat. They'll go so well with the dress you picked out for Izzie to give."

He groaned. "I've unleashed a shopping monster."

"That's why you should be careful what you wish for." She headed toward the front of the store. "And for the record, turtle eggs are all I'm qualified to mother."

Izzie's heart wouldn't agree. And frankly, neither did his. But with the clock ticking on the summer pilot program, he only had six weeks give or take to convince the turtle lady otherwise.

Chapter Nine

"Turtle watch tool kit? Check."

Caroline hefted the repurposed fishing tackle box filled with syringes, latex gloves, needles, tags and applicators. "Turtle-monitoring data sheets?"

Izzie held the clipboard aloft. "Check."

"GPS to record nesting locations?"

Max brandished the handheld device. "Check, Turtle Lady."

She bit back a smile. "Cooler with crushed ice to chill blood samples?"

Amelia raised her hand. "That would be me."

"Stakes, flags, measuring tape and spade?"

Her father shook the duffel bag clenched in his hand. "All here," Seth growled. "Is this really necessary?"

Some of Caroline's enthusiasm waned. Honey and Amelia had maneuvered him into partici-

pating in the turtle walk. She'd divided the seaside beaches among the grad students. Her team
would patrol the barrier island beach across the
tidal marsh from the Duer Lodge.

And under the students' leadership, the grat-
ifyingly large numbers of Kiptohanock volunteers—thanks to Reverend Parks—would cover
the beaches June through Labor Day on a rotat-
ing basis to mark nesting locations.

Caroline reminded herself she should be thankful her dad was here at all. But the night was
young. Plenty of time for him to get on her last
nerve and vice versa.

She returned to the checklist. "Laundry bag?"

Honey laughed. "As always, that would be me."

She was the main reason their father had finally agreed to come. With Sawyer working on
last-minute camp details and Braeden on Patrick
duty, Seth was strong-armed into watching over
Honey.

Caroline was used to Honey working her wiles
on their father. It amused her to no end, however,
that although he'd at first refused Amelia's and
Honey's attempts, he'd been unable to say no to
Sawyer's quiet request. Seth Duer had a real soft
spot for Honey's ex-Coastie.

"Don't forget about me." Weston's voice rang
out over the crashing surf.

As if she could.

"What exactly did you bring to the party, Commander Clark?"

His teeth flashed even and white in the darkness of the night. Caroline knew she amused him every time she called him commander.

"I brought the essentials of life, Dr. Duer."

"Which are?"

"Coffee." He removed the black backpack from his shoulder. "Energy bars and water in case sometime between midnight and 1:00 a.m. we need a snack break." He grinned at her again.

"Good thinking, Commander Clark."

Honey had the nerve to giggle.

Caroline ignored her sister. "Turtle watch party present and accounted for. Remember, no cell phones or other kinds of lighting. Turtles get easily confused and could head inland by mistake or right back out to sea instead of laying their eggs on the beach."

She surveyed her motley crew of family members and friends. This, she hoped, would be the first of many summers to come for newly inaugurated Kiptohanock turtle patrols. The success of the future rescue center depended on a community taking ownership. And nothing bred ownership better than an up-close and personal encounter with one of the majestic creatures.

The circle of life for real. And that especially applied to her curmudgeon father, whose endorsement she'd need with the all-important Watermen's Association meeting next week.

"Everyone can now switch on your red headlamp." Caroline demonstrated. There was a flurry of clicks and a pinkish red glow spotlighted the sand.

"Some nights we can expect three to four nesting females. Other nights?" She shrugged. "Nothing."

Her father scraped at his beard stubble. "Sounds like a long night to me. *For* nothing."

She prayed for patience. Reminded herself self-control was a fruit of the Spirit. And ignored him.

Caroline led the way across the beach. "Keep your eyes peeled for turtle tracks." She paused now and then to give tidbits of information.

"Sea turtles spend ninety-nine percent of their lives in the ocean. Female turtles only come ashore to lay eggs. The males never come ashore. Scientists know little of the behavior of male turtles."

"Could be said of humans, too." Her dad plodded through the sand. "Except we'd be talkin' the female of our species."

Under her breath, Caroline counted to ten. *Ignore him.*

She faced forward. "Only one egg in a thousand will produce an adult turtle. Gender is determined by temperature. Warmer waters produce females. Cooler temps result in males."

Weston attached himself to her elbow, matching her stride for stride. "So you're saying in Turtle World, it's basically hot chicks and cool dudes."

Max snickered.

She only just stopped herself from laughing. "That's certainly one way to look at it, Commander Clark."

He leaned close, for her ears only. "You're not fooling anyone with the Commander business."

She pursed her lips. "Sea turtles face two primary obstacles. First, coastal erosion with the loss of beachfront as sea levels rise and—"

Caroline rocked to a standstill. The group halted behind her. There, two hundred feet ahead in the sand. "Stay here," she whispered over her shoulder. "I see something. Let me check it out first."

Holding her breath, she crept up behind a dark shape. *Thank You, God.* She'd never have lived it down with her grizzly bear father if she'd wasted his time and his sleep. She hurried back to the waiting group.

Izzie bounced in her flip-flops on the sand. "Is it another turtle mama?"

"A leatherback. We'll move in for a closer look. But go quietly." Caroline touched her index finger to her lips. "We must speak softly so we don't interrupt the female's work."

Excitement bubbled inside Caroline. A perfect night. No wind and only the sound of the breaking waves. She gazed around at the expectant faces. Izzie and Max were about to explode from anticipation. Even her dad forgot to paint his features with indifference at the prospect of the egg laying.

Finally, she'd get to share *what* she loved the most with *those* she loved the most. She glanced at Weston. With the hard lines of his chest outlined in the untucked polo shirt, his rolled up jeans and bare feet, he seemed as attuned to Shore life as any local.

And yet there was so much more to Weston Clark than met the eye. Fluttery pleasure brushed her heart like the feathery wings of a dragonfly at the prospect of sharing this experience with him.

Weston loved seeing Caroline in her turtle lady element. The cool, detached veterinarian replaced by this extremely knowledgeable beach girl scientist. He'd seen her in action speaking to community groups in her classy business attire and in her lab coat and surgical scrubs at the marine hospital. But beautiful as she was, nothing, in his opinion, compared to Caroline in her well-worn jeans, *Save the Earth One Turtle at a Time* T-shirt and flip-flops.

He glanced at his daughter. Izzie wasn't the only one who'd caught hold of Caroline's excitement. The turtle lady's joy was contagious.

Loud sighs emanated from the massive sea turtle. Using her front and rear flippers, the turtle made the sand fly as she excavated a nesting pit.

Caroline had fallen to her knees in the sand beside the leatherback. Weston and the others clustered around the turtle he estimated to weigh close to eight hundred pounds. Donning latex gloves, Caroline crawled around on her hands and knees doing a cursory examination.

"So this is what a turtle lady does?" Seth's gruff voice had lost some of its sharpness.

Enlisting Amelia and Weston's help with measuring the turtle, Caroline gazed at her father on the other side of the turtle's carapace. "I spend my nights coated in sand."

She blew out a breath and dislodged the swarm of beach gnats worrying her eyes and nose. "Glamorous, isn't it?"

Her father harrumphed, a sound somewhere between agreement and admiration.

"Is it okay to bother the turtle mama?" Izzie whispered in reverent awe.

Caroline smiled. "It's fine. Turtles go into a type of trance while laying eggs."

With gauze she'd swabbed in antiseptic, she prepped the turtle's left flipper for blood collection. "We don't know for sure, but we believe leatherbacks can live up to sixty years." Caroline injected something the size of a grain of rice encapsulated in glass into the turtle's right shoulder muscle. "These are PIT tags."

At Weston's upraised brow, Caroline translated. "Passive Integrated Transponder tags." She ran a handheld scanner over the location of the tag. "We receive a low-energy radio signal by which we track and map their migratory habits, adding to our field of knowledge."

Seth shuffled his boots in the sand. "Caroline?"

A pulse throbbed at the base of her long, slim neck. "Yes, Dad?"

"I think you ought to know this location on the beach will be well below the high tide line come July."

She stared at him. "Thank you, Dad. That's very helpful to know. We'll need to relocate the nest once the turtle mama is done." She smiled. "You may have saved a hundred eggs from washing out to sea."

Her father pursed his lips and ran his gaze over the foaming waves behind them. "No problem."

A smile wobbled beneath his bristly mustache. "You're welcome."

For a split second, Caroline cut her eyes to Weston. Then she turned her attention to her sea creature patient. And Weston wanted to cheer for the tentative beginning she'd made with her dad.

Caroline lifted one of the rear flippers so everyone could peer inside the nest cavity. "I'll need that laundry bag now, Honey."

She and Honey tucked the cloth bag into the nest hole just as two billiard-ball-sized eggs plopped inside. Honey's eyes, like the way he imagined his own, were wide.

"This will give you a whole new perspective on your own future childbirth experience, eh, little sister?" Amelia teased.

"Max," Caroline instructed. "You and Izzie are in charge of keeping count on the data sheet."

Over the next hour, soft plunks and plops accompanied the turtle's labored breathing in the egg-laying process. When smaller misshapen eggs emerged, Caroline explained they were yolkless eggs. "False eggs, which indicate the laying is coming to an end."

The turtle suddenly shifted, using its front flippers to pivot.

Gathering the laundry bag, Caroline fell back onto her haunches. "She's covering." She peeled off her gloves.

"Final count." Max's eyes gleamed. "One hundred and thirty-two eggs." He clicked the pen against the clipboard. "Sixty yolks and seventy-two…" He looked at Caroline.

"Seventy-two fertile eggs." She ruffled her nephew's carrot-topped hair. "Great job, Max."

The turtle spent an additional forty-five minutes throwing, pushing and packing down the sand on top of the cavity to camouflage the nest. Weston reckoned the nest would be hard to spot once the tide washed away the tirelike tread of the turtle mama on her return to the ocean.

"Seems a shame, doesn't it?" Seth rubbed his jaw. "For the turtle mama to work so hard when her eggs aren't there anymore."

Izzie crouched nearby. "Why is the turtle mama crying, Caroline?"

"They're not tears. It's mucus, Ladybug."

Max's head snapped up. "I read in a book that some people believe the turtle *is* crying. Crying because she won't ever see her babies again."

Izzie gasped.

Caroline dropped to the ground beside Weston's daughter. Sitting cross-legged in the sand, she pulled Izzie into her lap. "Turtle mamas can't survive in this environment for sixty days, Ladybug. They have to leave."

"They don't want to leave?" Izzie wrapped her

arms around Caroline's waist. "But they have to, right?"

Max huddled into Amelia. "My first mother died..."

Seth placed his arm around Honey's shoulder. "Mamas never want to leave their babies, kids." Sadness passed across his face. "Took me almost a lifetime to understand it's not because of anything we did." His eyes bored into Caroline's. "Whether we're talking cancer or something else."

A look passed between Caroline and her father.

Weston sank down beside Izzie. "The turtle mamas have to be where God meant for them to be, Monkey Girl—in the water."

Caroline let go as Izzie crawled into his lap. They watched silently as the turtle mother, having spun completely round, plodded to the sea. The waves crested over the turtle mama's shell. And then she was gone.

Izzie sniffed back a sob and buried her face in his neck.

Caroline scrambled to her feet. "One other thing I forgot to mention, Izz. Mother turtles pass a genetic signature to their turtle daughters. And those daughters will return year after year as egg-bearing adults to the same beach where they were born. Isn't that wonderful?"

Izzie lifted her head. "I—I guess so. So the

turtle daughters always come home. Kinda like a turtle family beach reunion?"

Caroline's gaze slanted toward her father. "Exactly…"

"Eventually…" Seth agreed. But he smiled at his daughter.

And Weston's heart nearly exploded at the look that transformed Caroline's face.

Fighting the moisture dotting her eyes, Caroline hauled the egg sack to higher ground. "This high enough, Dad?"

Seth cleared his throat. "Reckon that might do."

"A stake will mark the spot." Her mouth curved. "Now who's ready to dig?"

Chapter Ten

"Car-o-line…?"

She clutched the cell phone to her ear. "Izzie, what's wrong?"

"Daddy burned the c-cookies…" Sobbing hard, Izzie hiccuped.

"I'm sure it was an accident. He didn't mean—"

"You don't understand," Izzie wailed. "Now I don't have anything to bring. Church ladies are s-supposed to bring something to the baby shower."

A fresh round of sobbing. "I'm a church lady, too." Further crying commenced.

"Izzie?" No response. "Isabelle." Caroline used her sternest professorial voice. "Let me talk to your daddy."

More hiccuping. "H-he can't come to the phone right now. He's running up and down the stairs in the lighthouse."

"Why in the world is he doing that?"

"Because he's mad at himself, he said." Izzie hiccuped. "And so he won't cuss."

Caroline held the phone away from her mouth so she could laugh.

"Izz—?" She regained control of herself. "You listen to me. You tell your daddy to bring you to the cabin. We'll whip up something before the party starts. How's that?"

The waterworks ceased as abruptly as the wind in the eerie calm in the eye of a hurricane.

"Really?" Izzie's voice quivered.

"You'd be doing me a favor. I'd completely forgotten about bringing hors d'oeuvres to the baby shower."

"We don't have to bring those oar-things. Just food."

Caroline smiled into the receiver. "Good to know, Ladybug. You've saved me from a Southern faux pas."

Izzie sighed. "I don't know exactly what that is, but I think Daddy made me try it once, and I didn't like it."

Tears of merriment rolled down Caroline's cheeks in her effort to preserve Izzie's dignity.

"I think you're absolutely right, Ladybug. No faux pas for us. But I have a great recipe we can make together. I'll text your dad the ingredients if you guys can stop at the grocery store on the way."

"Roger that, Caroline."

Caroline imagined the redheaded little girl saluting her in the smoky haze of the cottage kitchen. "See you soon."

"Thanks, Turtle Lady."

As Izzie clicked off, Caroline laid her forehead on the countertop, free to give in to her mirth.

Thirty minutes later at the sound of knocking, she opened the cabin door to father and daughter on the porch. Izzie waved. A grocery bag in each hand, Weston just looked sheepish. And endearing.

Caroline ushered them inside. Izzie—being Izzie—strode toward the kitchen like she owned the place.

"Is that a new cologne you're sporting, Weston?" Caroline sniffed the fabric of his shirt as he lumbered past. "I've got to say it's certainly a new scent for you."

She cocked her head and tapped her finger on her chin. "Smoky with hints of spice and overtones of…" She made a show of enlarging her pupils. "Oatmeal?"

"Ha-ha." But a smile played at the edges of his lips.

"Recipe gone wrong? Don't worry. It could happen to anyone." She stopped in her tracks for dramatic effect. "Oh, wait. This only seems to happen to you, doesn't it, Commander Clark?"

He moved so quickly she found herself pressed against the wall of the entryway, rimmed in on either side by grocery bags and his arms. A nervous giggle escaped from her throat.

"I told you from the beginning, Dr. Duer, cooking is not one of my more notable skills."

From this up close and personal, the blue in his eyes blazed, full of her. Her gaze flicked to the strong, angular line of his jaw. Beneath the palm of her hand against his shirt, she felt his heart hammering with a beat to match her own. And if he hadn't been halfway holding her up against the wall, she wasn't sure her knees could've supported her.

"And this, I'm guessing, is what you regard as one of your hidden talents, Commander Clark?" Her voice emerged husky.

The blue in his eyes went opaque. "Why don't you find out?" He drew closer till only inches separated his mouth from hers.

His breath mixed with hers. She inhaled. Her lips parted—

"Daddy! Caroline! Let's get this cooking show on the road," Izzie bellowed from the kitchen.

His head slumped forward to rest on the pine-paneled wall. "My daughter, the ultimate chaperone."

Caroline let a breath of air trickle between her lips. Then she laughed. "Coming, Ladybug!"

He released her from the circle of his arms. "Thank you, Caroline. This means a lot to Izzie."

"Don't thank me too soon." Caroline headed toward the kitchen. "I'm no Honey when it comes to cooking. But with this old recipe of my mother's, I think Izzie and I can hold our own with Kiptohanock's finest."

Plunking the bags onto the counter, Weston removed the ingredients.

Switching on the water faucet, Caroline washed the cucumber at the sink. "What were y'all trying to bake? Something really hard?"

Izzie dragged the counter stool to be beside Caroline. "Just the frozen pop-and-bake cookies from the grocery store."

Caroline tore off a paper towel from the roll. "And they let you command men, run a cutter and rescue people in the Coast Guard, *Commander* Clark?"

"When you say it like that, it sounds as if you doubt my abilities." He grinned. "You're not so bad at performing rescue operations, either."

She placed the cucumber on the cutting board and withdrew a paring knife from the butcher block. "So you're admitting you need a rescue?"

He leaned against the countertop. "I guess I am, and I'm not too proud to admit it. Long time coming, huh?"

Long time, indeed. For her, too.

Weston Clark looked way too good in his jeans and T-shirt. She found it difficult to stare at him, slice a cucumber and, at the same time, not lose a finger.

Izzie propped her chin in her hand. "What's this recipe called?"

Caroline's attention once more focused on not losing a finger. "Cucumber rounds. It's elegant party food."

"Whew!" Izzie blew out a breath. "Long as we're not making those foe pa thingies."

Faux pas? he mouthed.

Caroline's lips twitched. "No faux pas here, for sure. Not on my watch."

One thing led to the other and before any of them realized, it was time to dress for the baby shower. Weston went home to do a quick search and grab of Izzie's dress and other fashion accessories per Caroline's instructions.

She and Izzie disappeared into the one bedroom at the cabin while he finished plating the open-faced cucumber rounds. Which he nearly dropped when Caroline emerged in her brand-new party dress. He settled for his mouth dropping open.

"Wow." He made an effort to close his mouth. To be safe, he placed the crystal tray on the counter and out of harm's way.

Her dress was indeed similar to Izzie's, except an all grown up and amazing version. For once, she'd allowed her hair to remain loose and long, where it waved around her shoulders.

"You clean up very nice." And he could've kicked himself for the backhanded compliment. When what he meant to say was she looked incredibly beautiful as always, only more so.

"A step above my turtle T-shirts." She gave him an uncertain smile. "But Izzie is the star attraction."

She made a sweeping motion toward the bedroom. "May I present Miss Isabelle Alice Clark?"

Izzie's head popped around the doorframe before the rest of her followed. "Hey, Daddy."

"You look gorgeous."

Izzie touched a hand to the black silk headband. "How do you like my hair? Caroline fixed it." The red curls no longer frizzed, but artistically framed her small face. "Don't I look like a real church lady now?"

"A real lady is exactly what you are." He opened his arms but stopped. "Am I allowed to hug the tower princess or will that mess up your hair?"

Izzie looked at Caroline.

Caroline smiled. "I think hugs are always in fashion."

He swept his daughter into an embrace. "Thanks for everything, Caroline."

"My pleasure. It's been so much fun tapping in to our inner girly-girl, hasn't it, Izzie?"

"Women like us, Daddy, don't have to be either or."

"Either or what?"

"Girly or brainy." Izzie gave him a firm nod. "We are both."

"Yes." He made sure his gaze encompassed Caroline, too. "You are."

A blush stained Caroline's cheeks.

"Can I give you ladies a ride to the fellowship hall?"

"That'd be great, if you don't mind."

"What guy wouldn't be proud to escort two such lovely ladies to the party? Besides, a bunch of us guys are going to keep Sawyer company at the diner while you sip punch or whatever ladies do at these shindigs."

Five minutes later, Izzie squeezed into the seat behind the extended cab. Weston held the tray while Caroline slid her long, slim legs into the passenger seat and buckled the seat belt. He handed off the tray to Caroline and got in on the other side.

Signs posted on Highway 13 advertised the upcoming Wachapreague Fireman's Carnival next week. And he deliberately chose the roundabout way from the Duer Lodge to Kiptohanock. Izzie kept a running commentary going about her favorite foods and rides at the Virginia State Fair near Richmond, where her grandparents lived.

"What about you, Caroline?" Izzie paused for breath. "What's the best thing about the fireman's carnival?"

"It's been a long time since I attended my last fireman's carnival."

He palmed the wheel as he turned off the highway. "I doubt much has changed since then. It's one of the things I love about the Shore—how so much remains constant."

"Which brings problems of its own. Change doesn't always have to be bad." She gestured at the passing glimpses of ocean between fields of soybeans and isolated white farmhouses. "Like the marine rescue center."

"True," he acknowledged. "But constants such as family-focused, Eastern Shore friendliness make 'come heres like Izzie and me feel we've finally found a forever home."

"And then there's the food." Izzie's stomach growled as if on cue.

He caught Caroline's gaze, and they smiled at each other. He forced his eyes onto the road as they bumped over the small, picturesque bridge near Quinby. "My favorite is the ham biscuits."

"I like the cotton candy."

Caroline balanced the tray in her lap. "My favorite is the Ferris wheel."

Pulling into the church parking lot, he jumped out and made his way around to Caroline. Holding the tray aloft, he clasped Caroline's smooth hand in his and helped her alight from the vehicle.

Spotting Amelia and baby Patrick on the steps, Izzie ran over to greet them. "Patrick's not a lady. What's he doing here?"

Amelia fluttered her fingers at them. "His daddy's on duty, and his grandpa Seth is on Max duty."

Izzie squared her shoulders. "Right. 'Cause this is for ladies. Church ladies. Are you coming or what, Caroline?"

Amelia put a hand on Izzie's back. "Why don't we go ahead? I could use your help in getting Patrick settled before the rest of the guests arrive, Izz." She winked at Weston as she shuttled Izzie inside.

He'd always liked Amelia Scott, wife of a fellow Coastie. He loved Izzie to pieces, but time alone with the beautiful vet was hard to come by.

Caroline, he noticed, hadn't let go of his hand. And he didn't want to let go of hers, either.

"I guess I should go inside and make sure everything is ready when Honey arrives."

He needed to say something, but he was so out

of practice with this dating thing. Scarier than any rescue in the Bering Sea.

Caroline ran her tongue over her plum-tinted lips. "I appreciate the ride…"

Weston broke out into a cold sweat. This was way scarier than dealing with his drill sergeant at boot camp. He felt Caroline pulling her hand out of his grasp. His heart pounded. All she could say was no.

Not true. She could laugh. She could stare at him like he'd grown horns. She could shatter his heart into a million pieces.

"I'm sure I can catch a ride home with Amelia…" She released his hand and reached for the tray.

Maybe he misread the signals. Maybe she didn't like him at all. Not in a romantic way.

She'd said she wanted to be friends. Maybe her only interest lay in his motherless daughter. His pulse ratcheted.

He held on to the tray. She tugged. He refused to let go. She frowned at him. It was now or never. He took a deep breath.

"Would you go with me to the fireman's carnival Thursday night? Izzie's going with Max and Amelia. It would be just you and me." He gasped for air.

She blinked at him. "What?"

He gulped. "Just you and me." The tray in his hand wobbled.

She took it from him. He let her.

"You said that already." She pursed her lips. "Just so I'm clear, are you asking me on a date?" Her eyes narrowed. "Or are you apologizing for Izzie not being able to join our group?"

"No…" He swallowed. This was harder than he remembered. "This would be a date. If that's okay with you."

He had a sudden and horrendous thought. "You're not dating, seeing or engaged to someone, are you?" He held his breath.

She lifted her chin. "No, to all the above."

He exhaled. "That's good. And Thursday night?"

"I'd love to go to the carnival with you on Thursday."

He leaned over the tray she held between them. "And what I failed to make clear at the cabin is that I think you look fantastic in that dress. I think you are a wonderful person, too."

Caroline shook her head. "I'm not so sure about that."

"I am. I've watched how you're drawn to help the hurting—the turtles, my daughter." He stared into her eyes. "And me."

Something passed between them.

"Likewise, Commander."

"Caro—"

"In fact." Her lips curved. "If my sister, your daughter, the entire Kiptohanock church women's guild and townsfolk weren't watching us from the café and the fellowship hall..." She tilted her head down and looked up at him out of those big brown eyes of hers. "I might have even kissed you right now."

His heart skipped a beat as his eyes cut left and then right. She was correct. Genteel church ladies peered out of the fellowship hall window. And Caroline's male relatives plus half the Auxiliary were agog looking out of the plate-glass window of the Sandpiper.

"Rain check?" His mouth had gone dry.

She smiled and swept by him with the crystal tray. "Thursday. It's a date." Her sling-back pumps crunched across the gravel.

Weston threw a grin toward his Coastie compatriots at the café. Mission accomplished.

Chapter Eleven

Kiptohanock Banner—"Wednesday, June 17, after rehabilitation at the marine rescue center, six sea turtles will be released along the Kiptohanock shoreline at 10:00 a.m. The public is invited to attend."

Caroline kept careful watch as her grad students transferred the turtles to the tide foaming at her bare feet. A lot of teamwork had made this moment possible. The turtles—dubbed the Kiptohanock Six by locals—had been rescued and saved by having the marine center nearby.

On the waterfront in Kiptohanock, a crowd had formed to cheer the sea turtles' return to the ocean. Izzie perched on her father's broad shoulders and waved. Caroline's heart did a small trill at the warm light in Weston's eyes. A look just for her.

With effort, she refocused on the reason everyone had gathered. "First into the water—Ariel."

Caroline scanned the crowd. There, at the back of the ring of people, her father hunkered. "Ariel was accidentally hooked off the Quinby pier."

Placing the loggerhead under sedation, Caroline had successfully extracted the hook caught in Ariel's upper esophagus. With antibiotics and nutritional supplements, Ariel was now ready to resume her oceangoing life.

The grad students on each side of Ariel gently placed the turtle in the water. As the waves rolled onto the beach, the tide lifted Ariel and swept the turtle farther from shore. Everyone applauded.

Caroline gave the onlookers a brief rundown on sea turtles Snow, Belle and Elsa.

"You named 'em after Disney princesses? Gross…" Max pantomimed gagging.

She winked at Izzie. "Yes, I did. But once school starts, I'm giving the fifth grade dibs on naming the next round." The next three turtle princesses were released without incident.

"Aurora—"

Max gave a dramatic groan. Her father laughed.

"Aurora," Caroline continued. "Swallowed a large shark hook that was removed under sedation. Once the swelling went down, she began to eat well, and our veterinary staff cleared her for release."

Caroline stepped aside as her team transferred the final two turtles. "Tiana was reported hooked by a fisherman using a small J-hook, but no hook was observed when the Stranding Response Team arrived. Tiana's blood work and X-rays indicated no other health concerns. Tiana and the last turtle, Mulan, are Kemp's ridleys, the most endangered of the sea turtle species."

There were oohs and aahs.

Caroline waded shin-deep into the water. "Mulan was caught by a treble hook in the corner of her mouth."

She surveyed the crowd. "But she and the others are fine now, thanks to everyone who contacted the twenty-four-hour hotline and helped us rehabilitate these magnificent animals."

Caroline gestured toward the water. "All six turtles will carry an acoustic tag that transmits information about their ocean journeys. Adding to our scientific knowledge of their species, this will further ensure that there are sea turtles on the Eastern Shore of Virginia for generations to come."

Her father raised his hand as the last of the turtles found their sea legs—aka flippers—and swam away toward the deep. "And if a waterman encounters a hooked turtle, what should we do?"

"I'm so glad you asked."

Was her father finally thawing toward her and her life's work?

"Call the hotline and bring the turtle onto the dock or into your boat with a net. But do not attempt to remove the hook yourself. If possible, keep the turtle moist or better yet, in a shaded area until our response team arrives."

Amid more clapping, the crowd dispersed and the grad students repacked the gear. Weston set Izzie on her feet. *Tonight?* he mouthed.

Caroline nodded. Mixed degrees of anticipation and fear curdled in her stomach. With Max in tow, Weston and Izzie headed toward the library for summer story time.

Roland pulled Caroline into a hug. "Great job working the crowd. Your dad was perfect. Did you two rehearse?"

She made a face. "That would be a no."

As her father approached, Roland clapped the waterman on the back. "Your daughter is a treasure. You must be so proud."

She winced.

Her father glared at Roland from underneath his bushy brows. "Don't let us hold you up, Teague. I'm sure you've got somewhere you need to be."

Roland gave a nervous chuckle. "Sure. Sure." He made as if to move past Caroline. "This is why we need you, kid." He scuttled past. "Once a 'come here, always a 'come here.'"

Her father crimped the brim of his cap and adjusted it on his head. "You're good at what you do."

She waited for the other shoe to drop.

He folded his arms across his chest. "You've got a real way of inspiring people. And this turtle hospital is a worthy cause, I'll grant you."

But… There had to be a but coming.

"I'm still waiting to understand how a woman as intelligent as you could pour herself with such passion into these creatures, and yet walk away from your family."

Truth be told, Caroline was still waiting to understand, too.

"Your sisters have been over-the-moon now that you've come home after all these years."

"But not you," she whispered.

"You're after the Watermen's endorsement. And when you get it, will you move on somewhere else to enhance your résumé?"

For the first time in her career, Caroline knew she wouldn't. Not if someone asked her to stay. Someone like her father. Or Weston Clark.

When she didn't answer right away, her father's jaw tightened. "Consider yourself endorsed, then, daughter. Don't let me be the one holding you back."

"I don't want to leave, Daddy. The aquarium board has offered me a permanent position here on the rescue center staff."

He sighed. "For how long, though, before you get the urge to wander again?"

"I had to go." She clamped the bracelets against her side. "Don't you see? I couldn't survive and stay. And even then, I nearly didn't…"

He stiffened. "What does that mean?"

The old, dreadful blackness spiraled in front of her vision. Her breath accelerated. She'd been so busy this week she'd not taken her usual precautions. And with their semitruce regarding the egg laying last week, she'd not foreseen coming face-to-face with this particular trigger. Not today, leastways. She worried her lower lip with her teeth.

"Amelia knows." It was getting harder to breathe. "I—I can't talk about this right now."

If she could make it to the church sanctuary, slip in unnoticed, calm herself…center herself and pray…

"What concerns me are the casualties you leave in your wake." He snorted. "Weston Clark and his daughter don't know you as well as I do."

Her chest heaving, Caroline pushed past him. "I have to go."

Thank God Weston and Izzie weren't here to see her like this…

"You always have to go somewhere. Run away." Her father stepped aside. "After all, it's what you do best."

In a straight trajectory, she bypassed the Sandpiper and headed toward the church. Her hands shook as she thrust the sanctuary door open. Inside, she stumbled to the front, thankful that in Kiptohanock no one locked doors.

Caroline sank onto the first pew and practiced taking even, steady breaths. She thanked God the church was empty and no one around to see her humiliation. She quieted her heart and emptied her mind of the fear.

She'd discovered that sometimes the stress of fearing the attack could actually bring on an attack. So she focused on the altar cross for a long moment until gradually the anxiety receded.

Closing her eyes, she remembered the joy of the morning when the turtles had been returned to their natural habitat. She relived the grittiness of the sand beneath her feet and the tangy taste of the salt in the air. She smelled the brine of the ocean and felt the cool lap of the water against her shins.

And God was good. He'd given her satisfying, work to do that made a difference. He'd brought her back to her seaside home where first He called her heart to a noble task. He'd given her friends here—old and new. Allowed her a chance to reconnect with her family.

She grimaced. Maybe not all of them. But God had also brought a certain redheaded little girl into her life. Along with her incredibly handsome and altogether wonderful father.

"I don't deserve a future with them," she whispered to the cross on the altar. But instead of the doubt she grappled with on a daily basis, peace flooded the aching places of her heart.

And she realized with no small degree of amazement that for once, she'd fought off the debilitating despair. The darkness and panic had retreated. For now.

She suspected she'd always battle anxiety. But today, she'd prevailed. Turned what had been once upon a time an inexorable tide. And hope swelled. Hope for a new beginning. Despite what her father believed, maybe her future did lie here in Kiptohanock.

Hope and healing within the cradle of the Eastern Shore. An image of a little redhead and the child's ex-Coastie father rose in Caroline's mind. The thought of her carnival date with Weston tonight set her limbs aquiver.

Perhaps it was time to let someone in, to share the deepest wounds of her heart. She needed to tell him everything about her past. She was taking a chance, given his history with his ex-wife. But a real relationship had to be based on honesty.

Secrets destroyed trust. But with Weston, for the first time in her life, Caroline was willing to risk everything by telling him the truth. Because despite her fear of his rejection, shining more brightly was the hope she glimpsed in his eyes of what could be.

Weston couldn't stop his heart from pounding as he pulled to a stop outside Caroline's cabin. He'd already dropped Izzie off at the main lodge with Max and Amelia. Nervous, he reminded himself he'd been a commander in the Coast Guard. He'd rescued people and run a small cutter.

Now he wished somebody would rescue him from the palpitations gripping his chest. He'd been out of the dating scene for a long time. But it was more than that, he knew.

This woman stirred his senses and had him daydreaming of a new life. Daydreaming when he should've been sanding floors and prepping drywall. Daydreaming of a woman with whom at long last, his heart might find safe harbor.

At his knock, Caroline answered the door and as usual, blew his breath away in denim shorts, Keds sneakers and a T-shirt, which read *South-*

ern Couture. The miniature green turtles on the shirt sported pink bows.

She smiled. "Hey."

Weston leaned against the doorframe—mainly to recover. And tried for a studied, casual tone. "Hey, yourself. I like your shirt."

He cocked his head. "Like Izzie said. Not either or, but both."

Caroline laughed. "Thanks."

"Ready for carnival fun?"

She closed the door behind them and followed him to his truck. "Will it involve cotton candy and foot-longs?"

He held the door for her. "I could arrange that. Seeing as how I'm such a big spender and all." He grinned. "Next time I promise to do better."

If ever there was an open invitation... He reddened beneath the collar of his shirt at his unaccustomed forwardness. But Caroline didn't say anything either way.

Weston chose to take her shy, uncertain smile for an unspoken affirmative. No need to assume the worst. But he'd boarded drug submarines with less fear than embarking on this first date with a woman he couldn't get out of his head. A woman who'd taken up permanent residence in his heart.

They arrived in Wachapreague in time to see the sun set over the marina. She gave a big sigh. He turned at the sound.

"It's good to be home."

"You're happy here?" So much rode on her answer. Izzie's happiness and his. Their future.

Caroline smiled at him. Her face lit with a glow he'd not seen that first day they met at the library. A glow to which he hoped he'd contributed.

"Yes, I am." Her voice quivered. "I'm almost afraid to say it out loud. Afraid it might disappear."

He found her hand and gazed deep into her eyes. "Me, too. Happy and scared."

An impish smile hovered on her lips. "Only way to get over fear is to face it, head-on." She winked at him. "Together?"

"Why do I get the impression I'm going to live to regret whatever it is you have in mind?"

She batted her eyelashes at him. "I'm sure I have no idea what you're talking about. You're not scared of a little fun, Eastern Shore–style, are you, *Commander* Clark?"

His lips quirked. "Bring it, Turtle Lady."

"First, we need to eat before the cute kid contest begins."

"Aye-aye, Dr. Duer." He shuffled into line with Caroline at his side. "There's a plan to enjoying the carnival?"

"Like invading Normandy."

Amid the aroma of fried everything, he ordered a crab sandwich for himself and a hot dog for her. But selecting a picnic table amid Coastie friends from stations Wachapreague and Kiptohanock was his first mistake.

"Who's the pretty lady, Commander?"

"What ya want with an old sea dog like that, ma'am?"

She laughed. He huffed. The bantering continued as church families and Auxiliary buddies strolled past.

He rolled his eyes. "Maybe our first date in such a public place wasn't the brightest idea I've ever had."

She smiled. "I love the way you've made a place for yourself here on the Shore."

After they finished eating, he tossed the remains of their dinner into a garbage bin. "A walk on the beach after dinner at the Island House sounds like a better idea right about now."

"This is perfect." She threaded her arm through his and guided him toward the pavilion. "And I've got a surprise for you."

She pointed to the grandstand as a troop of frilly-frocked little girls marched onstage. Izzie, included.

"What in the world?"

His daughter waved.

"She wanted to enter the Little Miss Carnival Queen contest."

He pretended to groan. "Who is that carnival

princess up there and what have you done to my not-afraid-to-get-dirty daughter?"

She play-smacked his arm. "Not either or, re-member?"

"Why do I get the feeling my credit card has been involved?" He cocked his head. "And this is what she was doing when she went home with you after story hour this afternoon?"

"Girls' Spa Day at the Lodge. Honey did Izzie's nails. I did her hair. Besides, no pain, no gain."

"Why is the pain always in my wallet?"

She hugged his arm. "Getting beautiful doesn't come easy or cheap."

He hugged her back. "Wouldn't know it to look at you."

"Did you charm your way to commander?"

He brushed his lips against her ear. "You know it." And was pleased when she shivered a little at his touch.

"You'll be happy to know the dress came via Honey from a consignment shop in Cape Charles. Not so expensive."

"Duer women are a terrible influence on my child." He groaned for real this time. "And exactly why is my fearless, doughnut-hurling daughter embarking on the beauty pageant circuit?"

"I heard about the Battle of the Long Johns last year. But rest assured, Izzie's only doing this pageant because she wants to win the grand prize, an iPod. That and the sparkly crown." She laughed.

"You've created a monster, Caroline Duer."

But he was proud when Izzie—Isabelle Alice Clark, she informed the master of ceremonies—answered the questions and did her twirly thing on the platform.

The eight little girls took a seat in the chairs onstage while the judges tabulated the scores. Not to be outdone, Max—Izzie's chief nemesis and compatriot in the mischief department—competed for Little Mr. Carnival King.

When Izzie's and Max's names were announced as winners, the crowd went wild. The crowd being Weston, Caroline, Amelia and Braeden. As the children posed for pictures with the *Kiptohanock Banner* and *Eastern Shore News* photographers, Izzie hoisted her trophy above her head. Max followed suit with his trophy. The two of them resembled a pair of Olympic champions. After lots of hugs and kisses, Weston sent Izzie off with the Scotts to eat dinner.

"No sugar," Weston called after Braeden. "Or I'll never get her to go to sleep tonight."

Braeden smirked at him as he herded his family toward the food stands. "Same could be said for you, too, ol' buddy."

Weston flushed.

Caroline elbowed him in the gullet. "Now that your food has had a chance to settle…"

He crinkled his eyes at her. "That sounds ominous, Dr. Duer."

The sun's rosy glow had faded into the blue velvet dusk of night. Thousands of lights strung around the perimeter of the carnival sprang to life. A local band took center stage, and a soothing, thumping beat filled the air. Beach shag mixed with country twang. Foot-stomping fun.

If he could find his sea legs on a cutter in the Bering Sea, surely he could survive a dance or two without disgracing himself. He summoned his courage. "Would you like to dance?"

"Later." She pulled him toward an enormous, spiraling iron tentacle creature.

His eyes widened. "The Black Spider?"

"Chicken?"

He jutted his jaw. "Absolutely not." Which was kind of true. At least in regards to the carnival ride.

Whirling and spinning, she fell against him twice before he decided to make centrifugal force his friend. He pulled her tight against him in the seat. He was sorry to see the ride end.

She tugged him toward the carousel. "Let's catch our breath."

Caroline's essence filled his senses. "I have

a hard time catching my breath any time I'm with you."

She brushed his cheek with her lips. "Choose your steed."

His pulse did a staccato beat. "You choose for me."

She selected a white-painted steed with a flowing mane for herself. He mounted the black stallion next to hers. As the music began, the carousel creaked into motion. The flying horses came to life, rising and falling. The gear work rode up and down the brass rod.

Across the aisle, he offered his hand and Caroline took it. Hand in hand, they went round and round to the old-fashioned tunes of the calliope. He was taken aback at the sight of himself and Caroline in the mirrors.

He looked happy. Caroline threw back her head and allowed her hair to cascade down her back. His vision wavered like the dimples in the antique glass.

Could you fall in love on a first date? Somewhere between meeting for the first time at the library and tonight, had love already happened? Could this be the woman for whom he'd searched his entire life? Was God giving him a chance at love again?

Chapter Twelve

Caroline couldn't remember the last time she'd felt as carefree and happy. Maybe never. After the carousel, Weston bought cotton candy.

Later, they ended up on the dance floor amid other Eastern Shore couples beneath the twinkling lights of the carnival. But she saved the best for last—the Ferris wheel. They slipped into the seat as the carnival operator snapped the bar in place across them.

Upward, the car swung. They held hands as other passengers were loaded. Stop and then go. The car swayed. Up and over again.

Stars studded the night sky. The harbor lights glowed, outlining the harbor. Below, tiny beacons of light alleviated the darkness of the water and shoreline. Illuminating homes, where families lived together and loved each other.

From up here, she felt that she could see forever. Here, she could believe in forever. Love this man and his daughter forever.

Here, she could face another one of her fears head-on. As the counselor and the reverend had advised if she wanted to be free of the chains keeping her bound. To share with someone who mattered about the dark secret that haunted her.

God, help me. And dug her fingers into her palms.

She took a deep breath. "I have panic attacks, Weston. And I had a serious bout with depression."

He turned from his contemplation of their Eastern Shore world.

She fretted the bracelets on her wrist. "When my mother died, I was about to graduate from Tech. At the funeral was the first time it happened."

Caroline forced herself not to look away. To face her fear of disclosure. "I couldn't breathe. I couldn't think. The pain, the grief, was so bad I had to get away for fear I might die, too."

He sighed. "I know something about that level of grief." He draped his arm around her shoulders. "I can understand why you felt you had to leave."

"I wanted to die with her, Weston." She flung out her hands. "I had this overwhelming urge to throw myself in the open grave with her. That's when I knew I had to get away or…" She gulped.

He pulled her against him. In the solid buttress of his arms, his warmth, his strength enabled Caroline to say what she'd needed to say to someone for years.

"I was drowning emotionally. Daddy was lost in his grief, and my sisters were so torn up. I stopped calling because their sorrow only took me further into the black hole every time we talked. When I was offered a graduate fellowship, I moved farther away."

She knotted her hands. "As long as I kept working and didn't think about the grief, I managed to stay two steps ahead of the darkness."

"Did it help?"

"Only for a little while. But hiding—masking—what I was feeling inside, I did reckless things. Things I'm ashamed of. Anything to climb out of the hole." Her voice shuddered. "To escape the abyss. To feel better."

"If only temporarily."

She looked at him. A sea breeze ruffled his short-cropped hair. "I understand the empty places your wife tried to fill."

He tensed. "You're nothing like Jessica."

"Sadly, Weston, I am." She raised her eyes. "But I'm done with running. I hit rock bottom.

Three years ago, I scared myself and Roland's wife, Danielle. They forced me to get help."

"What happened?"

Dark fear and nausea churned in her belly, fighting with her desire to tell him the truth. Would he distrust her after she shared what she'd done? Honesty had forestalled any hope of a relationship she might have attempted in the intervening years with other men.

"I was hospitalized for a few weeks." She studied the sparks of light glimmering across the shoreline. "The doctors diagnosed me with clinical depression after…" She edged away and put space between them.

He held on to her arm, refusing to let her drift far. "No matter what you say, Caroline, I—"

She wrenched free. "You need to see what I did." She steeled herself and pushed the braided wristbands farther along her forearm. "I tried to kill myself."

Weston gave a quick intake of breath at the sight of the pale, thin scar on her arm.

Her heart jackhammered as she waited for his reaction. She felt in that moment as if her whole life hung in the balance. His next words might decide the course of the rest of her life. Forever.

"That's why you didn't come home, isn't it?" he whispered.

When she believed she might die from not

being able to see into his eyes, he looked up and caught her gaze. The compassion in his face almost undid her.

"But afterward?" he rasped. "Why didn't you come home later? Your family loves you. Family and God got me through what happened with Jessica."

"I was sorry as soon as I'd done it." Tears burned Caroline's eyes. "I was ashamed at how weak I'd been. How broken. But how could God love me when I couldn't even—" Her eyes flitted toward the distant horizon where the darkness and the ocean merged.

He touched her arm, lying upturned and exposed across her lap. "But to endure this alone…"

"You've met my dad and Amelia. The both of them, Duer tough. Which I am not. My family had enough to carry without having to deal with my problems. I've spent years in therapy confronting my grief and the past."

She bit her lip. "But I'm a lot better. The darkness doesn't come as often. Most times, like today, I'm able to avert the anxiety attacks. I'm so much better. Really well, Wes. Cured."

"Which is why you finally came home. Now."

"God gave me a second chance at life." She lifted her chin. "This last year, because of my rediscovered faith I realized I had to come home, if only to finally face the last of my fears. To make amends to those I've hurt."

"Caroline—"

"But I wanted you to know before you…" She dropped her eyes to the bracelets. "Before we went any further. So you could bow out before—"

The Ferris wheel swung into motion, and the car lurched. Both of them grabbed for the bar.

He pressed his shoulder against hers. "I'm afraid it doesn't work that way, Turtle Lady. I think I'm falling in love with you, Caroline."

"You shouldn't."

He pried one of her hands off the steel bar. "Too late."

"I'm so sorry, Weston." She quivered. "Just your luck, to always pick the crazy ones."

The Ferris wheel whirled into motion once more.

"Don't say that about yourself. I've told you about my past. The mistakes I've made. I'd never judge you for what happened. I have scars, too. They just aren't as visible."

"It's okay if you don't want to see me again. I understand."

That was a lie. She wouldn't be okay never seeing him again. But he didn't need to know that. This wasn't his problem. It was hers.

He shook his head and crushed her against

him. "It wouldn't be okay with me to never see you again. Nor for Izzie, either."

"Izzie…" Emptiness filled Caroline. "She deserves a real mother, not someone as scarred as…"

Both hands on her shoulders, he angled Caroline to face him as the wheel picked up speed. "I'm afraid you're it, Turtle Lady. She's already picked you."

Tears pinpricked Caroline's eyes. "I'm no good for her or you."

He took hold of her hand. His eyes never leaving hers, his mouth brushed the skin on her wrist. And his lips kissed her scar. Softly. Tenderly.

A thousand shimmering sensations exploded in Caroline's heart. The wheel completed another turn.

"Trust me, Caroline…" His hand caught in her hair, and his fingers rubbed a wisp of her hair between his thumb and forefinger. "Trust yourself."

His gaze traced the pattern of her features and lingered. "Trust us."

"Why would you want me in your life, Weston? I'm just a turtle lady. And far more damaged than any of my turtle princesses." The car rocked to a stop at the top of the Ferris wheel.

He cradled her face in his hands. "Because you're *my* beautiful turtle lady."

And his mouth found hers. His mouth tasted

of mint as his beard stubble sandpapered her cheek. But his lips, his touch, were gentle and undemanding. He paused, giving her time to pull away or not. Giving her the freedom to choose him. Or not.

Silencing her fears, Caroline leaned into him, placing her arms around his neck. And as the Ferris wheel carried them toward earth once more, she kissed him again underneath the glittering stars of her beloved Eastern Shore home.

Chapter Thirteen

Weston hadn't believed he could be this happy. As the next weeks flew by, he, Izzie and Caroline spent as much time together as work schedules allowed. Dinner at the cabin or lightkeeper's cottage. Ice cream at the Sugar Shack.

There were long walks on the beach monitoring the unhatched eggs. Izzie would race ahead. He and Caroline following at a more leisurely pace. Stolen moments at the top of the lighthouse in the lantern room. Kisses under the moonlight.

Late-night phone calls after he put Izzie to bed. He and Caroline shared their favorite movies and books. Talked about their music preferences. Spoke aloud thoughts on God. Gave each other glimpses into their souls.

Caroline also helped him pick out furniture for the master suite. As the days went on, more and more he pictured the lovely veterinarian becoming a permanent fixture in his home. Adorning his life and Izzie's. A helpmate. She'd already become a permanent fixture in his heart.

On a breezy morning in late June, Caroline pulled into the lighthouse drive and announced Turtle Mama was ready to return to her oceanic home.

"No…" Izzie's chin wobbled. "She can't go yet. Her babies haven't hatched."

He and Caroline exchanged glances.

Weston crouched beside his daughter. "We prayed for Turtle Mama to get better from her wounds and now she has. It's time for her to go home."

Izzie shook her head. Her hair flew around her shoulders. "Not without her babies." She pressed her lips together.

Caroline opened the hatch in her car to where Turtle Mama splashed in the kiddy pool. "I brought Turtle Mama here to say goodbye. I thought we could launch Turtle Mama from the beach where she was born. To where she'll probably return in a month or so to lay more eggs before the season's over this year."

Izzie planted her hand on her hip. "I'm not ready for her to go. I'm not ready to say goodbye." Tears gleamed in her eyes.

"Not goodbye forever." Caroline draped her arms around Izzie's waist. "Just goodbye for now. I've inserted a PIT tag into Turtle Mama. We can track her progress and follow her journey on the monitor at the lab."

"Mamas shouldn't leave..." Izzie whispered.

Caroline scooped the little girl in her arms. Izzie wrapped her legs around Caroline like the monkey girl he always claimed her to be.

Weston raked his hand over his head. "Izzie." He reached for her as Caroline's arms sagged with his daughter's weight.

"It's okay, Wes." Caroline lifted her chin. "I've got this."

She tucked Izzie's head into the curve of her neck. "I know how hard it is, Ladybug, to say goodbye to those we love. But we have to think of what's best for Turtle Mama and her babies. The sea is their real home."

Caroline's breath hitched. "Not here." She blinked and buried her face against Izzie's hair.

Weston smoothed a ringlet of hair from his daughter's face. "It's going to be okay, Izzie. I promise you."

His gaze drifted to Caroline. "We're going to be okay."

Izzie lifted her head. "I have an idea."

Dare he ask?

Caroline bit back a smile. "What idea, Ladybug?"

"I know how we should celebrate Turtle Mama's homecoming."

Later, he and Caroline once again maneuvered the Kemp's ridley to the beach beneath the dunes. As the tide washed over the turtle, Izzie tossed wildflowers one by one into the water.

Like a path to guide the turtle home. Reminding Weston of a Hawaiian "homecoming" he'd witnessed during his CG stint in the islands after a beloved local matriarch died.

As Turtle Mama disappeared beneath the waves of the sea, Izzie inserted herself between him and Caroline. Holding on to each of their hands.

"Goodbye, Turtle Mama," she called. "I love you."

And Weston found himself letting go. Of the pain and bitterness. Of the hurt Jessica caused.

It was time to emerge from his emotional hibernation. Today, with Izzie and Caroline by his side, at last he found the strength to say goodbye.

Enabling him to forgive Jessica for what she'd done and failed to do. To finally forgive himself for the hurt he'd caused Jessica. For what he'd done and failed to do. Seeing Izzie's mother with a compassion he'd been unable to find before.

In subsequent days, he felt a freedom he'd not experienced in years. A lightness of being. And an overwhelming peace.

Additional marine animals were rescued and treated under Caroline's pilot program. The land was acquired through grants and fund-raising to build the center in an abandoned fishery near the Kiptohanock docks.

For the first time in a long while, he felt a stirring of professional interest. He talked to his engineering partner about the possibilities. They submitted a bid and were awarded a contract to remodel the site in conjunction with a Tidewater-based architectural firm.

Caroline did a well-received children's story hour at the library on the ongoing battle to save endangered sea turtles. She and Sawyer discussed establishing a Turtle Week with the foster siblings next summer. And Weston?

Somehow he managed to finish restoring the original Fresnel lens in the lighthouse. Refracted through multifaceted prisms, the light pulsed like a star held prisoner by the glass. He couldn't wait to test it. He planned to surprise Caroline.

The lenses produced different types of beams. Flashing, fixed and occulting lights so that the periods of illumination lasted longer than the periods of darkness. An object lesson. An encouragement. An "I believe in you" statement of faith to the woman to whom he could no longer deny his feelings.

He loved Caroline. Plain and simple. Each morning as the sunrise pierced the dawn sky, his first thoughts were of her. And hers was the last face he visualized as he closed his eyes at night.

By now he'd figured out he had it bad. The idea of a forever life with Caroline and Izzie filled him with a joy and deep gratitude for God's goodness. To a man who deserved neither.

Caroline filled hollow places inside Weston. Not usurping God, but the places meant by God for a woman to fill. Healing on love's wings. A healing he prayed every day he'd help Caroline find, as well. She seemed to blossom before his eyes as the days passed. Perhaps his imagination or wishful thinking. But he thought not.

Caroline's eyes glowed with serenity. And he'd no need to look in the mirror to know his did, too.

Thank You, God, for this second chance at love. Thank You for never giving up on me when I failed You. Thank You for giving Izzie a mother who'll love her forever just like You.

A sunbeam freckled the floor. The illumined dust motes danced in cast light.

Suddenly, he knew with the remodeling nearly complete what he'd christen the lighthouse and keeper's cottage. *Heart's Desire*. Because God in His infinite grace had given Weston his.

She was not only better. She was well. Perhaps for the first time in her adult life.

Caroline felt good. Optimistic not only regarding mending broken family relationships, but also for a future and the hope of what God might have in store for her. Inspired by Izzie's courage, she was finally ready to confront the last of her fears. To face the grief. Let it go. And move beyond loss.

That afternoon, she left the lab and drove into Kiptohanock. She noticed her dad's truck outside the Sandpiper. But she turned onto a tertiary road, which led to the cemetery on a hill overlooking the fishing village and harbor.

She sat in the car for a moment to gather her thoughts and ready herself. Which was silly, actually. She was as ready as she'd ever be to say goodbye to her mother and sister. *Just do it*, she told herself.

Grabbing the bouquet of flowers she'd picked from the garden at the inn, Caroline got out of the car. She slipped into the quiet, iron-gated enclosure. A holy hush pervaded the cemetery underneath the cradling arms of massive live oaks.

She shaded her face with her hand. The barrier islands glimmered like a string of pearls in the blue-green waters where the inlet emptied into the sea. Peaceful, serene. Restful. Not unlike the glorious God-sized view from Weston's lighthouse gallery.

Taking a deep breath, she trudged past lichen-covered slabs and dodged the granite-speckled newer headstones. Pruitt, Keller, Turner, Colonna. Turnage. Savage. And... Duer.

Several generations of Duers, but Caroline stopped in front of her sister's headstone first. *Melinda Katherine Duer. Beloved daughter and mother. Gone too soon.*

Yes, she was. Yes, to all of it. She laid half of the flowers on the grave.

"I'm so sorry this happened to you, Lindi," Caroline whispered. "Max is such a good boy. Amelia takes wonderful care of him. He's very much loved and in him, we still have a little bit of you."

A blue jay alighted onto a magnolia branch. The bird's feathers were a brilliant accent against the smooth green of the leaves. A single tear tracked down Caroline's cheek. She faced the grave beside her sister's. And laid the rest of the flowers on the ground.

Marian Savage Duer. Beloved wife and mother. Gone, but never forgotten.

"Hey, Mama." She laid her hand atop the roughened edges of the monument. "It's me, Caroline. I know it's been a long time since I was here, but I wanted to tell you how much I still miss you."

She sank onto a nearby wrought-iron bench. "I'm so sorry for the mess I made with Daddy. I hurt him—" she grimaced "—and myself a lot.

I hope you'll forgive me, Mama. I'm not sure if Daddy ever will."

"I do forgive you."

With a quick turn of her head, she spotted her father at the edge of the Duer plot. "How did you know I was here?" She half rose. "I didn't mean to intrude."

"You're not intruding. I saw your car…" Her father sighed. "Do *you* mind some company on this pilgrimage of yours?"

She shifted a few inches, giving him room. "It is a pilgrimage, I guess. Long overdue."

He eased beside her on the bench. "Were you scared to come here, Caroline?" He laid one arm across the back of the bench. "Is that why it took you so long to come back?"

"Yes." She bit her lip. "But not in the way you probably think. As a scientist, I know better than most, nothing physical remains here of Mama or Lindi. I came mainly for me. I was scared of myself, not them."

She knotted her hands in her lap. "That makes absolutely no sense at all, does it? To talk to somebody who I know isn't there."

"It makes sense to me." Her father took her hand in his. "'Cause I've always believed those we've loved have merely gone on ahead. Out of sight yet closer than we suppose."

His gaze traveled across the grass to rest on

the twin headstones. "The essence of your mother and Lindi still exists. No longer sick. No more pain. Happy and well."

"Waiting for us to join them."

He looked at Caroline then. "But not before God's time." He shook his head. "Not before His time."

She exhaled, the sound coming out in a half sob. "But it seems like such a long time they've been gone."

Caroline blinked to clear the tears out of her lashes. "Some days, I didn't think I could bear to go another minute without them." She glanced at the sliver of blue sky above the trees. "Some days I didn't want to miss them anymore."

"I know. Me, too."

He adjusted the brim of his ball cap with his hand. "I had a talk with Amelia this morning. She told me how you watched over us from a distance. About the money you sent after the hurricane."

There was a subtle alteration in his voice. "And she told me what she suspects was happening with you while you were so far away."

"You know, don't you?" Her breath came in spurts. "You know what I did?"

Her father cradled her hand in his. The copper band gleamed in the dappled light cast through the tree canopy. He laid his hand over the band and the beaded bracelets.

"I want to apologize for not being there for you." He clenched his jaw. "I was locked in my own prison of darkness, and I failed to see how bad you girls were hurting. I should've been there for you. For Lindi, Amelia and Honey, too."

"None of what happened to me was your fault." She took a deep breath. "I did this to myself. You were not to blame. I was weak. I—"

"That's the real reason you refused to come home." Her father gripped her hand. "You were afraid we wouldn't understand. But I would've been the last to judge you, Caroline."

Her mouth trembled. "I was too ashamed to come home, Daddy. I wasn't there for you. Or Amelia or Honey. Or Max. I tried to take the coward's way out. Mom would've been so ashamed of me. I'm ashamed of me."

"No." Her tough, waterman father blinked back tears. "She wouldn't have been ashamed. She would've understood because she understood and loved me in spite of my own weakness."

Caroline drew back. "What are you saying, Dad?"

"When your mother died, you girls responded to her death in various ways. Lindi went looking for love in all the wrong places, as the song goes."

"But Amelia—"

"Amelia overcompensated by trying to be everything to everyone. She somehow believed if she could control everything, nothing bad would ever happen to her again." He made a face. "Control is another delusion. And Honey?"

Her dad scrubbed his hand over his bristly mustache. "Let's just say Sawyer could testify to her anger management issues before they found their happily-ever-after."

"But—"

"The point is, none of us is perfect, Caroline. And I was no help to any of you when I was lost in my own decade of sorrow."

He took off his cap and set it on the bench beside them. "Which unfortunately was not a new coping mechanism for me. Only this time when I mourned I didn't have your mother to help me emerge from the grief."

"What do you mean 'this time'?"

"You and me, Caroline, we're more alike than we're different. We feel things, some would say too deeply. We can't easily let loose of what we should let go of."

She fingered a woven bracelet. "I don't think you know what I—"

He stilled her hand. "I know about waking up to each day darker than the last. When everything is an effort. It's too hard to think. To make a decision. To leave the house. To get out of bed. To go on breathing."

She sucked in a breath.

"I'm talking about the kind of black depression that feels like nothing will ever get better. That *you* will never get better. When all you want is for the pain to stop any way you can arrange it. You're not alone in feeling this way. You're not the only one who's ever wished for oblivion."

She lifted her chin. "Maybe not, but I'm the only one of the Duers who ever tried to make it happen."

He took hold of her arm and tugged her to her feet. "I want to show you something." He guided Caroline toward one of the older headstones in the Duer family plot.

Kate Upshur Duer. Gone home. May there she finally rest at peace.

"Your mother, Dad?"

He nodded. "She is why I understand better than you could ever know."

"Reverend Parks said something once about her. But I'm afraid I'm the one who doesn't understand."

"I never wanted to burden you girls with the hard legacy I've lived with all these years. Fact is, maybe I should've told you, and then you wouldn't have felt so alone."

His chest rose and fell. "My father was what was commonly referred to in those days as a ne'er-do-well. He died incarcerated in prison after he stabbed a man to death over a woman in Norfolk."

"I didn't know that. But I still don't see how—"

"Because what he did influenced what happened later with me and with your grandma Kate."

Caroline touched his sleeve. "I'm sorry about your father, Dad."

"The Shore was more isolated in those days. I was scared to death one day the story would leak across the bay over to the Eastern Shore."

"Everybody still knows everybody else's business here, Dad."

Her father huffed in what for him passed for a laugh. "I was more afraid I'd grow up to be like him. A selffulfilling prophecy is a phrase I heard you use once about something else. Which is exactly why I never told a soul, except your mother, Sawyer and now you."

"Dad, you're nothing like that man."

He gazed at her. "Sometimes, my darlin', you and I are too smart for our own good. Too smart and yet so dense."

"I don't understand."

"Despite my being a naturally despondent, mixed-up young waterman, your mother loved me anyway. She told me because of God in me, I didn't have to become my father. Nor my mother, either."

He blew out a breath. "Though I've been less successful until recently with my mother's legacy…"

She studied the inscribed dates on her grandmother Duer's headstone. "She died when you were a teenager."

"Thing is, Caroline, my mother was a naturally despondent person, too. She lived in a state of fear and shame over the actions my father chose. She coped as best she knew how, running the family inn, raising her children, working in her garden. Pouring her heart into her quilts. She battled her pride and her hopelessness. But in the end…" He glanced away.

"In the end?"

"In the end, Caroline, after several unsuccessful attempts, she took her own life."

His words set off a seismic reaction in Caroline. A quivering from the marrow of her bones to her knees. Aftershocks of trembling. Her heart quaked.

Caroline wrapped her arms around herself. The sun had gone behind a cloud, and the wind off the harbor raised chill bumps on her arms.

She gulped past the boulder lodged in her throat. "You're telling me…" Tried again to speak and failed.

"We—you and I—share a genetic history of chronic depression." His blue-green eyes bored into hers. "If I'd come to terms with this sooner, gotten the help I needed sooner, perhaps I could've recognized the signs in you." He held her hands in his. "Perhaps prevented what you tried to do to yourself. I'm the one who's so sorry, Caroline."

Oh God, she was so cold. Why couldn't she stop shaking? What was wrong …

"I see…" She moistened her lips with her tongue. Her gaze fastened on the silvery ribbon of water far away in the harbor.

"Do you see? Truly?" Her father squeezed her hand. "Neither of us has to become her. Neither of us has to make the choice she made."

Caroline's dad took hold of her shoulders, forcing her to look him square in the eye. "Her mistake, I've come to believe, was she isolated herself instead of allowing her family, her God and the community to help her. She didn't have to die, Caroline. Neither do you or I."

Spots swam before her eyes. "If my doctor had known about my grandmother…"

If her doctor had known about her grandmother, she might yet be hospitalized. She might have lost her ability to practice veterinary medicine. And if she'd known about this genetic curse she carried in her mind?

She would never have come home. She would never have allowed herself to love Izzie and

Weston. Caroline shut her eyes. She would never have allowed them to love her.

"I hope you can find it in your heart to forgive me, Caroline."

Her eyes flew open.

"I love you, and I'm so glad you've come home to your family, who love you so much."

She stared at her father. A man of few words from a generation who'd been trained to conceal more than they revealed of their truest selves. A heart-to-heart was not his style.

Only his deep love for her, she realized, had prompted him to verbalize something from his past so deeply personal and painful. And noting the strain on his face, she—so much like him as it turned out and in so many ways—understood what the last few moments had cost him.

With an effort, she pulled herself together. "Thank you, Daddy, for telling me the truth. But there's nothing to forgive." Her hand touched his cheek. "I love you, too."

Her father enfolded Caroline in his burly arms. Her nose pressed into his shirt, she inhaled the scents of her childhood—the briny tang of sea air and lingering aromas of coffee from the Sandpiper. Everything good, loving and safe in Caroline's life.

"I know you've talked with Reverend Parks. He's a good man." Her father released her. "A man who rode the same dark waves we've strug-

gled against. And an example of one who's overcome. He's been a good friend to me."

She halfway expected the curtain of darkness
to descend again at her father's revelations. Or
at least, a shooting stab of pain from a stress-
induced migraine. But instead something else
came, maybe worse.

A seeping coldness. Shock, she guessed. Shut-
ting down her mind. Hampering her limbs. Closing off her heart.

"Daughter?"

She jerked out of her reverie.

Her father frowned. "This doesn't have to
change anything, Caroline. It can be a new beginning if we let it. A beginning to honesty and complete disclosure in our family. We'll call a family
meeting. No more secrets. No more shame. Only
light, and life, and healing."

But Caroline knew better. As she'd known that
long-ago day when she stood over her mother's
grave. This legacy meant the beginning of the
end. She wasn't cured. She wasn't ever going to
be well. There'd be only short reprieves from the
darkness.

Like a candle in the wind, the flame of her
wellness flickered and died against the onslaught
of the despair. The death knell to her dreams for
a future with Weston and Izzie.

The end of hope.

Chapter Fourteen

"It's time."

Standing a foot away from the flagging tape around the nest, Caroline wrinkled her nose at the telltale smell of eggs and wet sand.

Izzie's eyes widened. "Really?"

"See how the sand above the nest has caved a few inches?" Caroline pointed. "That's how we know it has begun."

Izzie danced, her feet bare on the sand. "The babies are finally going to be born."

"The hatchlings," Caroline corrected. "And don't get too excited yet. This could be a two-day process."

Izzie grabbed Weston around the waist and pulled him into her joy. "We're going to have babies."

He laughed and extricated himself from the impromptu duet. "What do we need to do, Caroline?"

She gazed out over the churning waves. "We don't interfere, but we can watch if you want. Nature must take its own course, though it's liable to be a long vigil."

Izzie tugged on his shirttail. "Can we, Daddy? Please?"

He shrugged. "Sure, why not? It's summer. No school."

Izzie gyrated with glee. She froze. "I need to get my journal and my camera." She spun on her heel and raced for the top of the dune.

He sighed. "Oh, for that kind of energy."

"The hatchlings once free of their shells will wait until the sand cools in the early evening to emerge. No hurry."

"You know Izzie. She'll be out here all day afraid she'll miss the party." A crooked smile lifted one corner of his mouth. "No reason the humans can't party, too. Hot dogs on the grill for dinner? Six o'clock?"

Caroline smiled as she turned toward the wooden steps. "I'll be here."

She didn't know how she was going to tell them about her plans. She couldn't stay here and allow Izzie to get more attached. Nor Weston, either, when she of all people knew there was no hope for a future together.

He followed her to her car. "We won't start the hatching without you."

"There are things, despite our wishing, we cannot change, Weston."

He cocked his head. "What do you mean?"

She scanned the exterior of the cottage, memorizing each feature for the lonely days ahead. "Things we have to accept." Her eyes swept skyward toward the lantern room at the top of the lighthouse. "Not everything is meant to be. No matter how hard we try."

The egg hatching freed Caroline to leave without breaking her promise to Izzie. And yet the thought of driving away, out of their lives, opened a hollow place in Caroline's life. A gaping wound. But far better to rip the bandage off now than to infect their lives with her mental instability and scar Izzie and Weston forever.

She dragged her gaze from the lighthouse to his face.

A frown puckered his forehead. "I'll speak to Izzie. Make sure she understands not all of the hatchlings will survive. Prepare her."

Sometimes the only way to make things better was to cut out the infection if healing were to occur. Someone else would become Izzie's mother. Weston—Caroline dug her fingernails into her palm—would find someone else to make him the perfect wife he deserved.

Caroline would never allow anyone to hurt them again. Least of all, her. But why did her life always have to be about leaving behind the people she loved?

"Tonight." The blue in his eyes sparked. "You'd better prepare for s'mores. It may get messy."

She swallowed and climbed behind the wheel. As far as her heart was concerned, too late. It already was.

"Watch how they go motionless to get their bearings," Caroline whispered.

On his belly flat in the sand, Weston regretted the third s'more he'd downed after dinner. Not to mention the two hot dogs before that. He groaned.

"Shh…" Izzie hissed, lying prone on the other side of Caroline.

"How do they find the sea?" he whispered.

Just outside the stakes, they lay in wait for the momentous event. The sun had set in a fiery orange ball over the shimmery edge of the world. In the indigo gloaming of early evening, a sea breeze set the flagging tape aflutter. Like his heart every time he got close to the gorgeous turtle lady.

"A scientific mystery for years." Caroline shifted. "We now understand they see the light above the ocean is brighter, lighter on the horizon."

His breath ruffled the mahogany tendrils of hair curling around her ear. "So you're saying they're drawn toward the light."

Caroline angled her head a fraction. "When you put it like that, yes." She wasn't smiling, though, and she edged farther away, out of reach.

His eyebrows arched, but his focus changed to the hatchlings as they surged forward once more. Their visual GPS fixed on the ocean within seconds.

"Daddy!" Izzie breathed. "They're moving."

Caroline's mouth pulled downward. "As a group."

He wasn't sure what had happened between Caroline and her dad yesterday afternoon. But since then, she'd become remote, unreadable and too quiet.

Weston threw her what he hoped was an irresistible smile. "Coasties learn early it's about teamwork. True of life, too."

But she kept her eyes trained on the hardy band of survivors trudging toward the open water.

He bumped her shoulder with his. "Just like us, they make it with a little help from their friends."

She bit her lip but didn't respond to his attempt at playful banter.

His throat constricted. Had a fateful confrontation with her father severed any hope of reconciliation? His gaze was drawn to the sand as the hatchlings climbed over sticks and skirted clumps of seaweed on their march to the sea.

Izzie wriggled with excitement. "Amaaazing…"

For a moment, Caroline's face softened and lost some of its bleakness. She kissed the top of Izzie's head. Caroline pushed herself to a kneeling position.

A knot formed in his gut. Something was wrong. He rose more slowly.

Izzie scrambled to her feet. "How do they make it out alive?"

Caroline brushed the sand from her jeans. "One hatchling wiggles free of the shell and this triggers movement in his neighbors until more and more break free."

Izzie shook the sand from her clothes like a dog shedding water. "How do they know which way is up?"

He and Caroline shielded their eyes from the flying globules of sand. He laughed. "Instinct."

Caroline nodded. "Somehow they know. There's a digging frenzy. They flick, scrape and scratch at the walls of the nest. The sand ceiling above them collapses."

She led the way toward the surf on the narrow path they'd staked to funnel the hatchlings to the sea. "The hatchlings rise like they're in an underground elevator to excavate the next layer of sand standing between them and freedom. Which is why it takes several days with plenty of stop-and-go."

His eyes riveted on the baby sea turtles as a

wave dragged the band of hatchlings backward and left them stranded on the sand. But a bigger wave followed and lifted them as one. With their flippers no longer touching sand, the survivors were caught by the undertow. The hatchlings were swept ten yards out to sea.

"They made it." Caroline's stiff posture relaxed. "After a few days, the hatchlings will be far from shore and beyond the reach of beach predators."

Izzie squared her shoulders. "We should launch the kayak, Daddy, and follow them to make sure they find Turtle Mama."

Caroline cut her eyes around to him. "Uh, Izz. We explained that the other day."

Izzie planted her hands on her hips. "Their mother wouldn't leave them behind on purpose. She's out there, waiting for them." She padded into the surf as if she meant to follow.

"Not too far," he called.

A silvery path of moonlight bathed the water from the shore to the horizon. Caroline closed her eyes as if basking in its glow. Or praying?

Silence roared between them. Awkward. Painful. Emptiness consumed him as realization struck.

The knot tightened in his stomach with a certainty of dread. "You're leaving again, aren't you?"

She winced and opened her eyes. "The pilot program ends—"

"You're leaving us?" His heart pounded. It couldn't be true.

"We never talked about—"

"I want you to stay." Something tore inside his chest. "I love you, Caroline."

She refused to meet his gaze. "It's not enough to want—"

"You mean I'm not enough for you to stay." His voice roughened.

He looked up quickly for fear Izzie had overheard. But she played just out of earshot at the edge of the tide.

"If I stay I'll only hurt you both."

His gut seized. "If you leave you're hurting us both." Fear exploded in his heart. "We don't have to rush things. We agreed to take it slow. With your new job—"

"I'm turning down the job at the new marine center. Izzie wants a mother. You need someone reliable and steady to be your wife. I am neither of those things."

He jutted his jaw. "Why do you always sell yourself short?"

"I'm a black hole that would suck the life out of you and Izzie, Weston." She fixed her gaze on Izzie. "I can't handle that kind of responsibility for another human being when I can barely take care of myself. I won't do that to you or Izzie. I can't be what either of you needs."

Anger flayed his nerve endings. "I love you. Izzie loves you. I've seen firsthand how much you love my daughter." He took hold of her arm. "Are you standing here telling me after everything we've shared that you don't love me? 'Cause I don't believe it, Caroline. I don't believe it."

She jerked free. "What I think I feel or don't feel doesn't matter. I'm telling you that you can't base a life on a future with me."

"You say you don't want to hurt Izzie and me. You're already hurting Izzie and me. What I think you really want to do is to protect yourself from hurting."

The wind blew strands of her hair across her mouth. And angry as he was, Weston wanted to smooth the tendrils out of her face. Hold her in his arms and never let her go.

"I'm not safe, Weston," she whispered as if she read his thoughts. "I'll never be that wonderful woman you deserve."

"Don't you get it, Caroline? There never has been or ever will be anything safe about love."

He straightened to his full height and towered over her. "Are you telling me then you won't give us a chance? That you don't love me?"

She lifted her chin. "I don't love you, Weston."

Her words pierced his heart. His mind drifted to the night on the Ferris wheel. Another starry evening at the lighthouse gallery. And even now her eyes said what her lips would not.

Weston shook his head. "I don't believe you."

"Please…" She bit off a sob.

"Stop lying. To yourself and to me."

His nostrils flared. "You think you can live your life safe if you don't love anyone or anything. That's a life I sure don't want to live. And if you were honest with yourself, you don't, either. But by the time you figure that out, I suspect it'll be too late. Too late for Izzie and me."

"I'm so sorry, Wes."

He crossed his arms across his chest. "You've gotten really good at saying that, Caroline. That and walking away."

"I wish things were different." Sadness flickered in her eyes. "I wish I was different."

He worked to prevent his voice from cracking. "With or without you, I mean to make a life for her and me with the help of God."

Raw fury seared his flesh. Fury at himself for trusting her. Fury at his own stupidity. For daring to dream.

"With you would be sweeter than I dare to imagine. But one way or the other—with or without you—I'm going to find my happily-ever-after."

Caroline's lips trembled. "Which is as it should be."

Anger was almost a relief. Keeping the pain at bay. "When are you leaving?"

"Tomorrow," she whispered to the wind.

He blew air from between his lips. "Can't wait to get away from us, can you?"

"It's not you, Weston." Her eyes pleaded for his understanding. "This is about me."

But she didn't want his understanding. She wanted his absolution for wrecking their lives. He hardened his heart. "Unfortunately, everything about you has become all about me and Izzie, too, Caroline. My mistake."

She swayed in the brisk breeze blowing off the ocean. "I told you from the beginning I couldn't offer anything more than friendship."

He pursed his lips. "More fool, me."

She flinched as if he'd struck her. "I'll call Izzie and say goodbye when I get to my apartment in Virginia Beach. I will always be her dear friend. I won't cut her out of my life—"

"That's no good for either of us. If you're not going to be a real, vital part of Izzie's life, it's better you don't contact her at all, ever again."

Caroline inhaled sharply.

"She needs to move on with her life without you."

And he somehow had to find a way to move on with his life without Caroline.

She reached for him. "But—"

He slid out of her reach. Her hand hung midair for a moment before she dropped it to her side. The look on her face...

Weston tightened his jaw. If he didn't get away from her this instant, he was going to lose control of his emotions. Give in to the grief of losing her.

He might not be enough for Caroline Duer, but he had enough pride left that he didn't want her to see how she'd broken his heart so completely.

"I think we've said about all we need to say to each other, Caroline. I think you should leave now. I'll explain to Izzie. Goodbye."

He wheeled and strode toward Izzie.

Placing his hand on the back of Izzie's neck, he drew Izzie's attention to the outline of a ship on the ocean's horizon.

Alone at the base of the dunes, Caroline stared at them, silhouetted against the night sky. Weston's broad shoulders were rigid. Izzie said something to him, but he kept their backs to Caroline as they faced the sea. She'd never felt so alone.

Caroline had a feeling she'd just made the biggest mistake of her life. Should she—?

She took a step forward, then stopped. It had to be this way. For everyone's sake.

Tears stinging her cheeks, she left them at the water's edge as a cloud shadowed the moonlight and darkness covered the deep.

Chapter Fifteen

"So you're really leaving?"

Her father stood in the open doorway of the cabin. Heaving a sigh, Caroline pushed past him, toting her suitcase toward the car. "I wasn't going to leave without saying goodbye."

"Why are you doing this, Caroline?" He dogged her footsteps all the way to the car.

She threw the duffel into the trunk and slammed the lid. "I know you probably won't believe me when I tell you I'm not running away this time. Despite how it looks."

He leaned against the vehicle, his long legs extended in front of him. "Then tell me what you're doing."

"I can't stay, Dad." She cupped the bracelets on her wrist with her other hand. "I promise it won't be like last time. I'll call every week. Write. Return for a visit when Honey's baby is born. But

I can't…" Her voice shuddered. "You of all people know why I can't stay here. I can't take the chance of…of…" She gulped. "A relapse. There will be a relapse. You and I both know that. Seeing me like that would scar Izzie for life. Destroy Weston for good this time."

"Caroline." Her father's face contorted with grief. "It doesn't have to be this way. There's no certainty of a relapse. It wouldn't be like last time when you were alone. You'd have your family. Weston and Izzie's love to help you."

"Oh, Daddy, I wish… How I wish…" Her vision blurred.

He opened his arms. She laid her forehead against the scratchy cotton of his shirt. She inhaled the familiar, always-longed-for scents of her childhood.

"I'm not running away from you or the family, Daddy. I just can't stay and watch Izzie find her forever mother or Weston take a wife." She lifted her gaze. "I can't bear that. I can't stay here if I want to stay well. Please." She fisted his shirt with both hands. "Please try to forgive me."

He cradled her face in his calloused, work-hardened hands. "Nothing to forgive, Ladybug."

She choked back a sob. He hadn't called her that since she was a little girl.

"I love you, Caroline." He pulled her into a fierce hug. "And this will always be your home."

She wrapped her arms around his waist. "I love you, too, Daddy."

"Alone is no good, sweetheart. Trust me, I know. Like with your baby turtles, family and community are vital to survival."

"I'll call my therapist today, I promise."

"Are you headed to Virginia Beach?"

"For now."

Her father released her. "Give me a call when you get across the Bay Bridge." The experienced waterman swept a practiced eye toward the sky. "Storm's coming and you know how your old man frets when his chicks are away from the nest."

She nodded and swiped the tears from her cheeks.

"Come home when you can, Ladybug. We'll always be here for you." His gravelly voice thickened. "Waiting and watching for you."

"You're wrong." Izzie hurled herself out of the SUV before Weston could bring the Chevy to a standstill. "Caroline wouldn't leave. She loves me." She rocketed out of the car toward the cabin.

He scanned the empty driveway and rested his forehead on the steering wheel. Izzie hadn't believed him when he told her about Caroline's departure. He'd tried explaining about Caroline's career and, in desperation, even her illness. Bringing Izzie to the deserted cabin was the only way he could think of to get Izzie to see the truth.

As for accepting the truth? He was still working on that one himself.

"Caroline?" Izzie pounded up the steps. "Caroline? Where are you? Caroline?"

He pushed open the car door and eased to the ground like an old man. He'd done this to Izzie. Seth had warned him. Yet Weston had believed he was smarter. Smarter than the people who had loved Caroline the longest. Why?

Because he was arrogant. So sure his deep feelings for Caroline were returned. That they'd finally found their soul mate in each other.

He shook his head. There was no such thing as a soul mate. Why was he so stupid? Women couldn't—shouldn't—ever be trusted.

Not with the heart of his child. Nor with his. What was so wrong with him that neither Jessica nor Caroline had been able to love him enough to stay?

Inside, Izzie's voice echoed.

Helpless, his hands stuffed in his pockets, he leaned against the clicking, cooling engine. Listening to the gut-wrenching calls of his beloved child. His jaw tightened. He'd never forgive Caroline for hurting Izzie like this.

No. That wasn't right. Had he learned nothing

from Jessica? He couldn't allow the bitterness to twist him up inside again. Hate and unforgiveness would in the long run only cripple him and by extension, Izzie.

"Where are you, Caroline?" On the porch, Izzie's voice ricocheted off the tree canopy surrounding the cabin. "I love you, Caroline. Come back. Please, please don't leave me."

He squeezed his eyes shut. Her pleas like the cries of his own heart. When he could stand it no longer, he plucked Izzie off the porch. In the shelter of his arms, he carried Izzie to the truck. She buried her head against his chest and sobbed.

"It's going to be okay, Isabelle." His voice quivered. He slid Izzie onto the seat and buckled her inside.

Coming around the truck, he threw himself into the driver's side. "Maybe not today or tomorrow. But I promise you, we're going to be okay."

"The turtles and Caroline are gone..." Izzie beat the seat with her fist. "You promised we were going to be okay then, too."

His stomach muscles clenched. "I tried to get her to stay, Izz."

"Like you tried with my mom?" Her eyes gleamed with tears and fury. "Maybe you didn't try hard enough with either one of them."

Weston jerked. How did she—? The knot in the pit of his stomach contracted, squeezing the air from his lungs. And he remembered last week when he'd caught her on his laptop. The out-of-the-ordinary trip to the library the next day.

He raked his hand over his head. And stared at his shaking hand. Izzie had an insatiably curious mind, not unlike Caroline's, to know. Whether it was in her best interests or not.

Izzie laid her head onto the armrest and cried. He wished for a moment he could stop being the adult so he could, too.

Thrusting the gear into drive, he bypassed the lodge. The cab was silent, except for the sound of Izzie's heartbroken sobs. Lost in the could-have-beens, he steered the truck toward the home he'd hoped to create with Caroline. Toward a future he and Izzie would now spend alone.

At the cottage, he allowed Izzie to slip from the truck without a word. She headed toward the beach. Like her dad, Izzie needed to grieve her loss in her own way. Heartsick, he made his way into the house. The home he'd never share with Caroline.

The torn-apart kitchen called for his attention. Emails awaited him in his office. He could bear the thought of neither. He found himself in the family room at the base of the lighthouse. His gaze fastened on the nautilus shell on the mantel.

As the mollusk grew, its body left the old chamber for a new, larger space. It walled itself off from the older chambers. But the empty chambers remained key to its survival. The chambers created a golden spiral and regulated the buoyancy of the living mollusk. And the cross section served as a reminder of how far the mollusk had come.

He peered up the circling staircase toward the upper stories. Like the nautilus, he'd hoped... He gritted his teeth. If only he could seal off the past as easily as the mollusk. If only he could've steeled himself from loving Caroline Duer, as complicated and multichambered as the nautilus.

Weston stormed up the curving steps past Izzie's room. At the sight of the frilly pink decor, he closed his mind to the joy of the day when he and Caroline had moved Izzie into her brand-new quarters.

Hurrying onward, he threw open the door to the master suite. Picking up the jar of seashells they'd collected one morning on the lighthouse beach, he flung the contents against the wall. The glass shattered. Shards and seashells flew across the bedspread Caroline had helped him select.

"Will I always be alone?" he shouted. "Is this my punishment for not being there for Jessica?"

Seizing the photo he'd framed of Caroline and Izzie taken in front of the cottage, he shook it at the ceiling. "Punish me. Not Izzie."

As he tossed the picture onto the bed, his gaze

darted. Every square inch of space held memories of Caroline. He didn't know how he was going to live here with the images of her laugh and her face everywhere he turned.

"Why did you bring Caroline into our lives if you knew she'd never stay? Was it a test? That I failed? Again?"

Silence greeted him. His anger spent, anguish swelled. He sank to the floor beside the bed and put his head in his hands. His heart was shattered. He ached for the woman who would never be his.

But in the quiet, he became aware of the distant roar of the waves. The in and the out. The rhythmic cadence stilled the angry torrent of his thoughts. Calmed and regulated his breathing.

Vast. Unfathomable. Altogether more than him. Like God's love for him and Izzie. And Caroline, too. He lifted his head. "I can't do it anymore, God. I'll never be enough for anyone. I'm so alone."

The wind whistled against the brick tower. And in the caw of a seagull, his heart quickened with a realization. He'd never be enough, not on his own. Only God could enable him to be the father Izzie needed.

Only God could help Weston become a husband someday. Or, if not God's will, God would help Weston bear the tasks He'd set before him. But Weston would never be alone.

He recalled what Caroline had told him of the most terrible time in her life. Truthfully, he couldn't comprehend that kind of loneliness. There'd always been his parents, his sister and now his Kiptohanock friends and church community.

The anger toward Caroline seeped slowly from him. Replaced by a growing compassion for the burden she carried and the battle she was so determined to fight alone.

He prayed for God to heal their hearts, especially Caroline's. To help her understand she never had to be alone again. Not because of Weston. But because her Heavenly Father would never, never leave his child alone to face the dark.

Then he bowed his head and wept for everything the darkness had cost them.

Chapter Sixteen

Weston's stomach growled, and he jerked from where he'd fallen asleep beside the bed. It had been a long night after the hatching when Caroline walked away on the beach. And today even longer as he tried to comfort Izzie in the face of Caroline's abandonment.

He grimaced. Caroline had made no promises. She'd been up front from the start. If anyone was to blame, it was him for unrealistic expectations and allowing Izzie to get her hopes dashed.

Weston scrubbed his hand over his face. Propping one arm against the mattress, he hauled himself to his feet. He blinked at the brightness outside the windows.

His belly rumbled. What time was it? His gaze flew toward the digital clock on the nightstand. He sucked in a breath. Three o'clock. Neither he nor Izzie had eaten lunch. He couldn't believe he'd fallen asleep and slept for over three hours.

Like father, like daughter, Izzie wasn't one to miss a meal. Even if lunch in the summertime usually consisted of peanut butter sandwiches and watermelon.

He stopped outside her bedroom. "Izzie?"

No answer. He grunted and continued toward the gutted kitchen. He expected to hear the blare of the television, but when he crossed into the cottage, there was nothing.

"Izzie?"

His voice echoed in that unmistakable way in an otherwise unoccupied dwelling. Maybe she was still on the beach. His pulse accelerated. He shouldn't have left her out there alone so long.

Reminding himself Izzie was nine years old and not a baby, he started for the door. But he stopped and stared at the empty spot where the garden tomato Miss Jean had given them used to sit upon the windowsill. He wheeled into what was left of their makeshift kitchen.

A dirty paring knife and cutting board lay inside the steel sink. He did a quick survey. The loaf of bread was smaller than he remembered from yesterday. A banana, a bottle of water and two granola bars were missing, too.

Izzie had probably given him up as lost and done lunch without him. No need for panic. But his heart ratcheted a notch. Maybe she was having a picnic on the beach right now...

Quickest way to check, he tore through the cottage and headed once more up the lighthouse staircase. Outside her closed bedroom door, he paused as another thought struck him. When he'd mounted the stairs earlier, hadn't Izzie's door stood open?

"Izzie?" His fist pounded the door. "Answer me, Isabelle."

He thrust the door open. It banged against the wall. He strode across to the window overlooking the beach.

The waves piled high, churning and foaming with a coming storm. The sky had darkened in the brief time he was downstairs. But there was no redhead in sight.

He crossed to the opposite window overlooking the tidal estuary. Nothing. Wait...

An orange life vest haphazardly lay between the rocky point of the Neck and the water's edge. But the kayak—

He inhaled and counted the rack on the shoreline one more time to be sure. As if you could somehow miscount between two kayaks. One kayak was gone.

Dear God, no. She couldn't have been that foolish. She's spent her life, young as it is, on the water. She knows better. Where is she going? What is she after?

He fell against the windowpane. Izzie knew better, but the heart? The heart wants what the heart wants. Her words from the previous day replayed in his head. She'd gone after the hatchlings.

In a sad, desperate sort of way, he understood his daughter's motivation perfectly. She might've lost her mother, and she'd lost Caroline, too. But Izzie would make sure—no matter what—the hatchlings didn't lose theirs.

He straightened. She couldn't have gotten far. God help him, his little girl couldn't have traveled far. But into the open ocean? His heart quailed.

Panic streaked through his veins. His chest heaved. Black spots danced before his eyes. He couldn't seem to catch his breath. Pain stabbed. Was he having a heart attack? Was this what it was like for Caroline when she suffered one of her anxiety attacks?

Oh, God. Help me find her before it's too late. Keep my precious child safe.

And he reached for his cell phone.

Caroline hadn't realized it'd be this hard to leave.

She procrastinated, making an excuse to drop by her office one last time. To say goodbye to her grad students bound for home after this summer's internship. But she skipped Roland's office and his not so subtle attempts to get her to reconsider the job offer.

Hands on her hips, she scanned the holding tanks and contemplated what the team had accomplished in a few short months. The directorship of the new facility would've been a plum assignment for a professional seeking to keep her hand in the game and yet make room in her life for the next chapter.

She swallowed, hard. But marriage and motherhood would never be in the cards for her. Not now. Not ever.

"It's for the best." Her voice floated across the empty lab. "Really it is." She worried her bottom lip in her teeth. "Isn't it, God?"

Not expecting an answer, she removed her lab coat, draped it across a stool and made herself walk out of the building to her waiting car.

With a heavy heart, she soon found herself circling the Kiptohanock square in the SUV. One more time, she told herself. Goodbyes were part of recovery. Necessary for letting go and moving forward.

Caroline drove past the Sandpiper, where her sisters had taken Max and baby Patrick for a consolation lunch. Because the Shoreside Duers were feeling down about her abrupt decision to return to her old job in Virginia Beach.

The church steeple pierced the darkening sky. Dad was right. A storm was coming. She'd best quit lollygagging and get herself over the Bay Bridge before driving became hazardous. Yet she idled the car outside the library. Recalling the curious day she met Isabelle Alice Clark. And Izzie's father.

Her heart thumped. Only two months ago? Why did it seem like so much longer? As if maybe her life began from that moment.

"Stop it." She banged the wheel with the palm of her hand. "Just stop it."

Without further ado, she peeled past the library and toward the highway. No need to stop at the cemetery. She'd made her peace with the unchangeable. Her mother and Lindi weren't there. Just the shell they once needed, but no longer required. Like her hatchlings.

At the memory of the hatchlings—Izzie's hatchlings—Caroline's eyes welled. Izzie was just beginning to break out of her shell, too.

But so many hazards remained on the way to Izzie becoming everything God intended the intelligent, little redhead to be. Caroline jolted as the car clanked over the small Quinby bridge.

A process—the thought stabbed anew—she wouldn't be around to witness. Nor to guide or encourage. Weston would have to navigate the tricky, turbulent waters of the adolescent years alone.

But perhaps not. She turned onto Highway 13 and pointed the car south. Perhaps Weston would yet find the one, true love of his life. A partner, a helper, a soul mate.

She blinked against the treacherous tears sliding down her face as rain peppered the windshield. He deserved a good woman to love him as Caroline could not. Someone to be there with him and for him as the years rolled by. Filling the beautiful home he'd created with life, laughter and love.

Choking hard with sobs, she fumbled to turn on the windshield wipers. How could she be so selfish to begrudge his ultimate happiness? Even if it meant with someone other than her. Because it had to be with someone other than her.

She took one hand off the wheel to dash the moisture from her cheeks. Her leaving was the right decision for everyone. The only outcome possible given the curse she carried.

But oh, how her heart ached with every mile separating her from those who'd become dearer than her own life. She scowled. *This was what came from loving people.*

She'd believed she'd learned that lesson when her mother died. If you never love anyone, no one can ever hurt you again. But instead she hurt herself.

A car honked as the SUV accidentally drifted into the adjacent lane. Cringing, she pulled herself together. Was that what she was doing now? Hurting herself by not allowing anyone to love her?

She readied herself for the certain onslaught of the darkness. Steadied her hands. Prepared to pull off the highway when the panic attack came.

Emotional stress was her trigger. Entering Northampton County, she gripped the wheel as the farmland and railroad tracks flashed by on either side of the highway. Ready as she'd ever be for the breath-stealing, fear-induced anxiety to commence.

But nothing happened, although the sadness at her leave-taking remained. An aching, inconsolable hollow in the pit of her stomach, which neither the miles nor the minutes seemed to abate, much less cure.

Her mouth trembled as she slowed to a stop to pay the Bay Bridge toll. She *was* better. At least, today. She'd made the right decision in leaving when she did. Hadn't she?

She crept forward in line with the other vehicles. Who knew what would've become of her if she'd given Izzie and Weston her whole heart?

Images flashed across her mind of a white dress

trailing in the sand below the lighthouse. Her family flinging birdseed at her and a handsome ex-Coastie commander groom. Izzie scattering rose petals to the wind—

She gasped. Of all the crazy ideas, surely the craziest of them all.

Get it through your head—she gritted her teeth—*there's no future for you there.*

She cut her gaze to the rearview mirror. She looked a sight. Her red-rimmed eyes puffy, her makeup streaked across her face.

Pulling up to the attendant in the booth, she fairly flung the money at the woman's outstretched hand. The woman's startled look softened as she hit a button inside the booth to lift the bar blocking Caroline's escape.

Escape? She chewed her lip. Was that truly what she was doing? Again?

"Godspeed, my friend." The attendant's warm brown eyes held Caroline's. "Wherever you're headed, Godspeed."

Crossing Fisherman's Island was a blur. Keeping on her side of the narrow lane in the strip-lit tunnel proved an exercise in willpower.

At the end of the second tunnel, she emerged into the brightness of the light. Pulling the car out of traffic, she parked in the lot of the Chesapeake Grill on one of the four man-made islands in the midst of the watery expanse. Silencing the motor with a flick of her wrist, she vacated the vehicle. The rain had passed for now. Yet as in life, another squall loomed on the distant horizon.

Bypassing the restaurant, she headed toward the pier with views overlooking the bay. Seagulls cawed and swooped overhead. The wind whipped her ponytail into disarray.

Her arms folded across the railing, she peered at the rocks surrounding the immense bridge pylons where the waves crashed. Was this what her return to Virginia Beach was about? Escape.

Was she still running? Had her life been about escaping her family? Or all along, was she trying to escape herself?

She laughed. The wind snatched the sound and carried it away. Who was she trying to fool? There was no escape from oneself.

Her gaze skittered to the rocks below. Nor there, either. A fragment of Scripture floated through her mind.

If I climb to the sky, You're there! If I go underground, You're there!

One of the verses Reverend Parks had shared with her. One of his greatest comforts, he'd declared in his own struggle against the melancholy. She'd liked the contemporary, everyday version he quoted to her.

Is there anyplace I can go to avoid Your Spirit? To be out of Your sight? She sighed. *If I flew on morning's wings to the far western horizon, You'd find me in a minute—You're already there waiting!*

Reverend Parks had encouraged her to memorize the psalm. Part of the mending of her spirit, he said.

The storm clouds billowed across the sky. She shivered as the wind picked up speed. No matter where she went, *she* and her problems would always be there.

But so would God. With her when the next relapse came. Her father's brusque voice whispered in her mind. *If* her next relapse came.

If... Suddenly, a word laden with hope.

"What should I do? I don't want to hurt them." Her breath caught on a sob. "I'm so afraid of being hurt myself."

But she'd also inherited more than the depression from her family, she realized. And she gathered the remnants of the courage her mother had displayed in her fight against the cancer that stole her earthly life.

Caroline garnered the fortitude of her father's faith, which carried him through the hardest of times—the deaths of a beloved wife and child, through illness both physical and mental.

As for her faith? She squeezed her eyes shut and swayed as the wind buffeted her body. Did she trust God enough to risk loving Weston and Izzie?

She'd turned the car around to head north and just passed through the turnstiles at the toll plaza when her phone buzzed on the console. One hand on the wheel, she frowned as she retrieved the cell, recognizing the number. She'd missed three calls while out on the pier.

Her father hated modern contraptions like cell phones. He maintained nobody needed to be in touch 24/7. He only used his cell in the direst of emergencies.

She tucked the cell between her shoulder and neck. "Daddy? What's wrong?"

"I know you said you'd call when you reached your apartment. I'm sorry to bother you, but..."

Her nerves quivered. "That's okay, Daddy."

"I thought you'd want to know."

"Know what?" An inexplicable fear took hold.

"Izzie's gone missing, Ladybug. She took one of the kayaks, and Weston can't find her."

Her heart drummed in her chest.

"We figure she's gone after those turtle babies of hers."

Sharp, unrelenting pain stabbed Caroline's heart.

Caroline yanked the car off the road and into a gas station lot. "He's contacted the sheriff? And Braeden at the Coast Guard station?"

"Everybody's looking for her. Reverend Parks has organized a team of volunteers to help the sheriff's department comb the woods between the lighthouse and Kiptohanock."

Her father's voice cracked. "Max is beyond distraught. What if somehow she's already slipped past them and hit open water?"

"There's a storm coming, Daddy," she whispered into the phone.

He groaned. "Storm's already here."

With a crackle of static, the call dropped. And the connection bridging the gap between Caroline and her father broke.

Chapter Seventeen

"You can't stop looking for her." Weston grabbed hold of Braeden's arm. "We've got to find her. Suppose it was Max?"

Braeden's gaze never wavered. "I'd be going as crazy as you are right now, Wes. But we've done everything we can until this storm cell passes. The choppers from Air Station Elizabeth City are grounded and so are we for the duration. I'm sorry."

Weston shook his head. "She's out there." He gestured toward the sheets of rain pelting the Coast Guard station. "She's lost and alone. We have to do something."

A flash of lightning lit the darkening sky. Weston jolted. Thunder boomed, shaking the building. The electricity flickered.

"No way we can risk venturing out in this until the worst is over, Wes."

He pounded his fist on Braeden's desk. "By then, it could be too late."

Seth touched Weston's arm. "Braeden's right. It's too dangerous for the search party to keep looking right now."

Weston gritted his teeth. "I can't sit here doing nothing while my child is out there."

"Izzie is more likely to head home since the storm has intensified. Somebody needs to be there for her." Seth held up his gnarled hand at Weston's motion of protest. "Best thing you can do is wait it out at home."

Braeden nodded. "I promise you as soon as it's humanly possible I'll have my guys back out there searching for her."

Seth steered Weston to the station lobby. "I'll get the *Now I Sea* on the water, too. Lots of tidal creeks meander off the inlet. It wouldn't be hard for a youngster like her to get turned around."

The waterman clamped a hand on Weston's shoulder. "She may be only a few miles, as the seagull flies, away from home right now. Hunkered somewhere safe. Taking shelter till the storm passes."

Lightning crackled, splitting the sky open in a dizzying array of ozone-charged particles. Weston and Seth both flinched.

Weston gulped past the boulder lodged in his

throat. "And if she hasn't beached the kayak? If she's on the water?"

Seth's eyes glimmered. "I was wrong before. Best thing you and anyone can do at a time like this is to pray. Pray hard." He gripped Weston's forearm. "But none of us will give up looking. Not till she's safe in her bed this very night, son."

Caroline did what she should've done fifteen years ago at the first sign of trouble—she went home. From Northampton County through Eastville, Nassawaddox and Exmore, she drove and prayed for Izzie to be found. Radio reports warned of flash flooding on the secondary roads off 13.

Home. Home. Home.

The rain beat the refrain onto the car roof. It took her entire focus to keep the car on the highway amid the torrential downpour. Wind gusts rocked the SUV from side to side.

As summer thunderstorms went, this was a bad one. Hands locked around the wheel, she cringed at the violent shotgun blasts of thunder overhead. When traffic snarled around Painter, she beat the wheel with the palm of her hand.

"Come on. Come on." Vehicles ahead came to a halt. "Get out of the way and let me through."

The windshield wipers worked at a frenzy. Creeping forward, finally, she reached the turnoff for home. Only to find the tiny bridge at Quinby washed out. Not a good idea to go through water in a car, but she had to get to Izzie. She had to get through. Izzie needed her.

Caroline clenched her jaw. Why hadn't she seen it earlier? Izzie needed her, but more importantly she needed Izzie in her life. Sending up a swift plea for mercy, she drove the car into the water. The rear tires spun, losing traction. Her heart raced.

The car lurched forward. Her breath hitched, but the car climbed out of the water to dry ground on the other side of the bridge. Bypassing Kiptohanock, she soon pulled into the Duer driveway. Yet the house lay dark and appeared deserted.

Her hands fell from the wheel, and she shrank into the seat. No one was home. She'd been so sure she was supposed to come here, but what now? The rain sounded upon the roof of the car like a hollow drum.

At the top of the driveway, headlights flashed. Momentarily blinded, she threw out a hand to shield her eyes. But to her overwhelming relief, her father's Silverado parked alongside.

The truck cab dinged. An interior light blazed as her dad thrust open the door. Slamming the door behind him, he tromped over to her car. Swathed from head to toe in his neon-yellow water slicker and black Wellington boots, he rapped his knuckle against the window. "Caroline?"

Catching the handle, she pushed open the door. "Have you found Izzie, Dad?"

"What're you doing here? You're supposed to be in Virginia Beach."

Rivulets of rain drenched Caroline, soaking her T-shirt and waterlogging her jeans. "I had to be here, Dad. For Izzie." She shivered.

He angled himself to shield her from as much of the rain as he could. "We haven't found her yet. The search was called off until the storm passes."

"Where have you looked?"

He tugged Caroline toward the deep-planked porch of the inn. "Let's have this conversation out of the rain."

Sheets of rain funneled off the eaves of the house. As her dad outlined the areas already searched, a growing certainty gripped Caroline.

"I know where she is, Dad."

She clutched the sleeve of his coat. "I showed Izzie on the computer the track for Turtle Mama's PIT tag. Deep underwater, the turtle's gone stationary to recover her strength as is typical after egg laying."

"Out to sea?" Her father shook his head. "If Izzie's out there... No one could survive out there on a night like this, Caroline. Especially not a nine-year-old 'come here in a kayak."

"Not on the open water, Dad. There was a shoal. The last sandbar before the channel widens and spills into the ocean."

"High tide's soon." His mustache bristled. "That strip of land will disappear with the tide and beneath the storm waves if it hasn't already. She'll be trapped if she's taken shelter there."

"I have to go." Caroline lifted her chin. "I can't leave her out there."

Her father seized hold of her hand. "You can't go out there. You won't make it."

"I won't make it without you. Help me, Dad." Rain lashed her face like a thousand stinging nettles. "Please."

A half smile softened his weather-roughened features. "Never could resist a stray, could you, Ladybug?"

He raised his chin a fraction, too. "All right, daughter of mine." Pulling her into a quick, fierce hug, her father kissed her forehead. "Let's go."

Caroline slipped and slid down what had become a mud pit toward the dock. Discarding the flip-flops, she joined her surefooted father on board the *Now I Sea*. She untied the mooring lines as he cranked the engine. But the motor sputtered and failed. He exchanged a worried look with his daughter.

She steepled her hands under her chin. "Please. Please. Please."

He tried again. The engine whined but sparked to life. And she released the breath she hadn't realized she was holding.

Not a pleasure boat, the tough little workhorse chugged away from the dock and into the tidal marsh. She stole a glance at her father behind the wheel. Seth Duer knew these waters like the back of his hand. If anyone could get them safely through these extreme conditions to rescue Izzie, it would be him.

The waves sluiced over the sides of the boat. She staggered and would've fallen except for her dad catching her arm.

"Sit down!" he shouted above the wind as the boat rocked. "Strap yourself in."

Caroline sank onto a seat nearest the center mass of the boat and folded her arms around herself against the cold. Buffeted by the rain, he rummaged in a storage locker and tossed a rain slicker to her. "It'll keep the wind off you."

She shuddered every time the lightning cracked across the sky. Struggling to make headway, nevertheless the *Now I Sea* chugged resolutely onward. Caroline kept lookout as the boat neared the location of the shoal.

"There." Her father jabbed his finger at the upside-down kayak floating past the bow. "It's empty."

She bit her lip. "Hurry, Dad. Hurry."

Her father tightened his jaw. "Can't go much faster or we'll swamp the boat and flood the engine."

They were running out of time, and she knew it. She prayed as hard as she'd ever prayed in her life they'd find Izzie on the shoal. Suppose the kayak had overturned in the water with Izzie inside?

Oh, God, please no. Help us find her safe. Help Izzie to be okay.

"Caroline!" Her dad nudged his chin toward a small elevation of land in the vastness of the raging water.

Arms wrapped around her updrawn knees, a tiny figure huddled in the middle of the rapidly diminishing sandbar. Her face hidden, the child's red hair reflected brown in the pouring rain.

The waterman cut the throttle and slowed the vessel. "I can't get any closer, or I risk grounding the boat." He dropped anchor.

"Izzie!" Caroline clambered to the bow. "Isabelle."

The wind caught and swallowed her words, but Izzie raised her head. Her mouth pulled down at the corners, she squinted into the watery horizon. Caroline waved frantically.

Izzie rose in one fluid motion. "Caroline!"

Stripping off the rain jacket, Caroline grabbed a life vest before jumping into the water. She flinched at the sudden cold. She sloshed through the waist-high water and fought her way toward the sandbank. The gravelly silt cut the bottom of her feet as she found a foothold onto dry land.

Caroline opened her arms wide as Izzie ran toward her. The child clasped Caroline in a stranglehold. "Are you okay, Ladybug?" She lifted Izzie's chin and examined her features.

"I thought you'd left me forever..." The little girl sobbed. "You didn't say goodbye. I couldn't find you."

"I'm so sorry, Izzie. I'm here now. I'm so sorry I left you." She peered at the worsening storm. "We've got to get you out of this, Ladybug."

Kneeling, she helped Izzie into the life jacket. "We'll have to swim to the boat, honey."

Izzie recoiled from the churning waves. "I can't." She quivered. "I'm scared..."

"It's going to be okay, I promise." Caroline clicked the buckle in place. "Climb onto my back, Monkey Girl."

The child twined her legs around Caroline's torso and held on while Caroline staggered to her feet. Caroline struggled toward the water's edge. She prayed the water would help her carry Izzie's weight, and keep them buoyant.

Izzie gasped in shock as a wave washed over her bare legs. Her arms tightened around Caroline's neck.

Caroline lifted her chin and plowed forward. The water was already deeper and more treacherous since she'd reached the shoal.

She lost her footing.

"Caroline!" Izzie screamed.

They plunged underneath the water. Caroline scissor-kicked and jerked them skyward. Izzie had swallowed a mouthful of water and coughed. The child moaned.

"I won't let you go, Isabelle. Not ever," she whispered in Izzie's ear.

Caroline's father threw a life ring out to them. In relief, she grasped hold. "We made it, Monkey Girl." She shifted Izzie off her back, holding the little girl in her arms.

But when Caroline tried disentangling Izzie's death grip from around her neck, Izzie panicked and squeezed harder. "No, no, no…"

Caroline felt her strength ebbing. "I'm right here, Izzie. It's okay. I'm not going anywhere. You have to let go, just for a second."

Izzie cried and hung her head.

"Please, Ladybug…" Caroline breathed. "The special word, remember?"

Izzie's head snapped up. Her liquid blue eyes bored into Caroline's for a moment, searching Caroline's face. Then Izzie loosened her grip, allowing Caroline to insert the life preserver over her head.

Dog-paddling, Caroline shoved the ring through the waves toward the idling boat. Her father reeled in the lifeline, hand over hand, drawing them closer to the vessel.

He hauled Izzie onto the dive board and into the boat. Dripping water, the child stood trembling as he tugged Caroline on board. She'd no sooner found her footing than her father collapsed against the railing.

Reaching for him, she felt her heart staccato-step. "Dad? Are you all right? Dad?" He wasn't a young man. He'd already suffered one nearly catastrophic heart attack several years ago. Izzie held on to Caroline's shirttail as if holding on to life itself.

"I'm okay." He scrubbed the pelting rain out of his face. Grasping the side of the boat, he leveraged himself upright. "Thank You, Lord," he grunted. "Just in time." He gestured.

Pivoting, she watched as the waves washed away all traces of the shoal. That could've been Izzie...

Her father enfolded Caroline and Izzie in a wet bear hug. "God's never early, but always just in time." His beard shadow scraped Caroline's face as he kissed her cheek. "Ain't that so, Daughter?"

She closed her eyes and relished the feel of her father's embrace. "It is, Daddy. And thank you."

He released her and patted Izzie's head. "Don't thank me yet. It's going to be harder to return home than it was to leave."

With her arm around Izzie's shoulder, she followed her father to the wheel. "Isn't it always, Dad?"

Amid the pouring rain, her father's blue-green eyes—like the waters of the inlet on a blue-sky day—crinkled. "Not so hard when home is where the people you love, love you back." He turned his attention toward the controls.

Warmth flooded the hollow places long empty in her heart. With Izzie on her lap, she sank onto the seat nearest her dad. She wrapped the rain-coat around them both in an effort to share body heat and fend off the wind.

The blackness of the night and the driving rain obscured the shoreline. Dropping her gaze to the deck, Caroline blinked. The boat was taking on too much water.

"Dad? The boat… The water…" She motioned.

Grim-faced, her father fiddled with the maritime radio. He raised the mike to his mouth and pressed the button. Static crackled. "Mayday. Mayday. This is the *Now I Sea*…"

Tucking Izzie into the curve of her neck and cradling the crown of her head, Caroline sent out her own version of mayday to their Heavenly Father.

Because the road home had never seemed so long. Or as perilous.

Chapter Eighteen

As the hours ticked by and the storm continued to rage, Weston fought his own private battle with despair.

He grappled with overwhelming fear and hopelessness. The blackness of the night outside the lantern room windows reflected the bleakness of his heart. And magnified the insidious, seeping doubt he'd never see his beautiful child again.

Was this what it was like for Caroline? He could hardly breathe for the inner turmoil lashing his heart. He fell to his knees in agony.

He'd always believed himself strong of mind and body. But how had the fragile Caroline coped with this kind of anguish? And for years?

Weston prayed with every ounce of his being for Izzie to come home to him. And if she didn't? He sucked in a breath at the suddenness of the thought—he'd want to be with her no matter what.

He shook his head against the idea. But he wondered whether, if he'd been given to melancholy like Caroline, he'd be so easily freed from the dark notion. If perhaps this was a taste of what she'd endured and overcome in her war against the darkness.

The phone in his jean pocket trilled. Clumsy with emotion, he dug it out with trembling hands. Good news? Or the worst?

"Weston? This is Braeden."

He swallowed against the lump lodged in his throat. "Have you found Izzie?"

"She's with Seth Duer, Wes. He and Caroline found her."

"Thank You, God," Weston breathed, and then frowned. "Caroline?" He clenched the cell.

"We received an emergency transmission from Seth on the *Now I Sea*. With the storm, visibility is at zero. He's lost onboard navigation and barely powering through the storm. There's no way to pinpoint his location until the squall lifts."

"You've got to get to them," Weston growled into the receiver.

"I'm afraid it's not that easy, Weston. No one is safe venturing out on the water right now. The storm won't lift till morning."

"We can't leave them out there in the elements." His voice rose. "If they lose power completely, they could be hopelessly lost, drifting," His heart sank further. "Dead in the water."

Braeden sighed. "I know. But there's nothing we can do right now, except trust them to God."

An idea dawned.

"There is one thing…one thing I can do to bring them safely home." Weston clicked the phone off. "And I will with God's help."

Over the roar of the wind and waves, Caroline clutched Izzie and sang snatches of an old hymn she remembered her mother singing on stormy nights long ago. Something about a love that didn't let go.

"You see me in the dark." Caroline's teeth chattered. "Darkness isn't dark to you."

Izzie tilted her head. "What?"

Caroline tucked the raincoat closer around Izzie. "It's from a psalm. 'At night, I'm immersed in the light. Night and day. Darkness and light. They're the same to you.'"

At the wheel, her father wrestled against the forces of the storm.

Izzie's cold, damp hand cupped Caroline's cheek. "I love you, Caroline."

Caroline's eyes pricked with tears too long held, further blurring the night. "I love you, too, Izzie." Her voice hitched. "So much."

The engine strained against the power of the wind.

Caroline chewed her lower lip. "I'm sorry, Dad. So sorry for getting you into this."

Her father softened his rigid stance. "No need to be sorry for anything, Ladybug."

"Ladybug?" Izzie shifted. "That's what Caroline calls me."

He laughed. "Two ladybugs you are. Two peas in a pod." He laid his hand upon Caroline's head.

She closed her eyes against the pummeling rain.

"No need for any more sorrow, Ladybug." His voice subtly altered. "There is a light that drives out the darkness."

Her eyes flew open.

"It's the lighthouse." Izzie gestured at a beam of light starboard side. "We're almost home, Caroline."

As Caroline's father steered the boat toward its source, the light grew stronger, brighter. She and Izzie held hands.

"Mind the rocks on the point, Dad," she cautioned.

Her father made a rumbling sound in his throat. "Best you stick to your turtle business, Turtle Lady, and leave me to mine."

Good ol' Dad. She thanked God some things never changed. Like His great love and the love of her family.

"Clang the bell, Isabelle," the waterman shouted as he cut the throttle and edged the *Now*

I Sea into the lighthouse dock. "Let yer dad know we've come."

Bouncing out of Caroline's lap, Izzie rang the clapper mounted at the bow of the boat. The sound echoed through the darkness of the night. Light spilled across the ground as a door was wrenched open in the cottage. A man stood silhouetted in the doorway.

"Daddy!" yelled Izzie.

Caroline caught Izzie around the waist before she plunged overboard in her haste. "Hold on, Izz. We're nearly there." She scrambled off the boat onto the dock and caught the mooring line her father tossed.

He eased the boat closer. "Better tie her down good."

"Izzie!"

The child's head snapped around at Weston's voice. Caroline's dad stepped out of the boat and helped Izzie maneuver across the gap.

Weston raced toward them. The rain flattened his hair. His shirt clung to his chest. But he had eyes only for his daughter. He gathered Izzie in his arms. "Izzie, baby." He feathered her bedraggled locks with kisses. "Sweetheart..."

And she hugged her daddy as if she'd never let go. "I'm sorry, Daddy. So sorry."

Caroline busied herself with the lines. Almost

her exact words to her father. Her eyes darted to the waterman.

A suspicious line of moisture tracked down his face. Swiping at his grizzled cheekbone, he snorted at her upraised brow. She smiled and grasped his hand. But she understood.

For Weston and Seth—at last their prodigals had returned home.

A pucker creased Izzie's brow. "I'm in big trouble, aren't I, Dad?"

His mouth trembled for a second before he regained control. "Yes, Monkey Girl, you are." He cleared the hoarseness from his voice. "But tonight we won't talk about that." He hugged her close. "Tonight we'll celebrate."

Weston faced Caroline's father. "I can never thank you enough, sir, for saving my little girl."

"I piloted the boat. It was Caroline who figured out where she'd gone."

For the first time, Weston focused on Caroline. "Thank you, Dr. Duer." He scowled. "I guess this means I owe you, too."

Sucker punched, she felt her stomach knot. But what had she expected? Her leaving had set this near disaster with Izzie into motion. Weston had every right to hate her.

Her father draped his arm across Caroline's shoulders. "I'm right proud of my girl here, son.

As pleased to have her back as you are to have yours home."

Caroline's heart thudded.

Weston's gaze flicked between Caroline and her father. "Come into the house and get dry. I'll let Braeden know to call off the search."

Her dad nodded. "And I'll get Sawyer to run out here first light to fetch us with the boat trailer."

"Good." Without another word, Weston turned on his heel. Izzie in his arms, he plodded up the rocky causeway toward the cottage.

Staring after them, Caroline slumped against her father.

"No question you love that little girl." Her father blew out a breath. "Real question is, do you love Izzie's dad, too?"

"For his sake, Dad, I wish I didn't."

He took hold of her chin and raised it level with his gaze. "For your sake, I'm glad you do."

"Dad—"

"Weston Clark's had the worst sort of day, daughter." He drew her toward the cottage. "Thought he'd lost the woman he loved and his child, too. He's confused and hurting. Give him time to adjust."

She hesitated at the bottom of the stoop. "Maybe I should keep my distance."

"Don't be afraid of what you feel. Don't be

afraid to love him, Ladybug. Just get in there and show him how much you love them both."

"What if—"

He shook her arm, none too gently. "What if Weston refuses to forgive you? What if he sends you away forever? So what if worse comes to worst?" Her father glowered at her.

Tough love, Seth Duer–style. But he was right. Facing the fear circumvented the anxiety and dealt a deathblow to depression.

She lifted her chin. "Then I guess I won't ever live in the lighthouse."

"Could be."

She planted her hands on her hips. "But I'll still have my family."

"That's for sure." Her father raised his face to the pouring rain. "But what else, Ladybug? What else you got?"

Caroline stamped her foot on the rocky soil and winced. She'd forgotten she was barefoot. "Then I'll still have my turtles, and my nephews will probably become the most spoiled children in the history of the world."

She tossed her head. Less effective with wet strands of her hair slapping her cheeks.

"There's my girl. Duers don't quit, do they, darlin'?" He laughed. "Go on."

He tugged her up the step. "Give that Coastie

what for." She stumbled through the open door and across the threshold.

Weston's shadow filled the doorway. "Ex-Coastie."

She froze.

He grimaced. "An ex-Coastie dealing with a born here, 'been here who doesn't have enough sense to come in out of the rain."

Before Caroline quite knew what hit her, Weston scooped her into his arms.

Weston carried her into the cottage. "Stubborn, know-it-all..."

She nudged her chin at her father. "Could use a little support here, Dad."

Caroline's dad wrenched the door shut behind them. "I think you've got enough support." He winked at Izzie wrapped in a blanket in Weston's recliner.

"Not enough sense to wear shoes in a storm..." Weston deposited Caroline on the sofa.

"D-daddy?" she stammered.

"Totally agree." Her father shrugged. "Common sense ain't that common."

She blinked. "Seriously?"

Weston towered over her. "Bleeding all over my hundred-year-old floors..."

Sure enough, a bloody footprint at the door marred the hardwood floor. The one step she'd taken before being abducted by this Coastie.

Her father chuckled. "Head always in the clouds. Or in a book."

She shot him a scathing glare. Her father rolled his tongue in his cheek.

Weston nodded. "Must be why she's so smart."

Caroline flushed. "Too smart for my own good?"

Weston's eyes flashed. "Izzie assures me she's okay. She's going to her room to get a hot bath." He scanned her father's wiry form. "You and me are about the same height. You need to get out of those clothes before you catch pneumonia. Feel free to use the phone in my room, too."

Unfastening his dripping slicker, her dad hung it on a peg inside the door. "I don't aim to catch phew-monia."

Izzie laughed.

"It'll take more than a summer storm to best this old sea dog." He looked at his Wellingtons. "What about—?"

"Best get to it, Mr. Duer." Weston's stern countenance didn't alter one iota. He tapped his shoe against the hundred-year-old floor. "I'll deal with Caroline. I've got a few choice things to say to her."

She shrank deeper into the cushions. Weston's face was about as ominous as the thundercloud currently hovering over the Delmarva Peninsula.

Throwing off the blanket, Izzie hopped out of

the chair. "I'll show you the way, Mr. Seth." She held out her hand.

"Mr. Seth's" eyes ping-ponged from Caroline to Weston. She couldn't be sure, but she thought she saw his mustache twitch. "Sure thing."

Caroline's eyes widened. "But, Dad..." What she wanted to say was, *Please don't leave me here. Take me with you.*

Her father saluted Weston as he and Izzie squelched toward the lighthouse stairs. They disappeared from sight.

Caroline's heart sank to her bare toes. And then cringed. Spots of blood also dotted Weston's hitherto white rug.

She scowled. At the rug. At her feet. At him.

And what she actually said was—

"You're real good at giving orders, aren't you, Commander Clark?"

He leaned back, his arms folded across his chest. Those true-blue eyes of his glinted. He clamped his jaw tight, a muscle jumping in his cheek.

And Caroline's heart skipped a beat.

Chapter Nineteen

The pipes squeaked overhead as Izzie filled the bathtub with water. With Seth also occupied upstairs, Weston studied Caroline, unsure how to reach her. Unsure how to tell her everything in his heart.

She crossed her arms over her wet shirt. Her hair hung in disheveled hanks to her shoulders. "I must look like a drowned rat."

He hunched his shoulders. "Even drenched, you're still the most beautiful woman I've ever known."

She blushed. Not what she'd expected him to say? His chest ached with the desire to cradle her. But first, he had to know.

"Why did you come back, Caroline?" He rocked on his heels. "Did someone call you about Izzie?"

"Yes, but no..." She shook her head. The hair

flew into her face and covered her features. "I mean…"

Because he couldn't help himself, he crouched beside the sofa and brushed a wisp of hair from her forehead.

At his touch, she stilled.

"I'd already turned around on the Bay Bridge and was heading home to Kiptohanock when Dad called," she whispered.

He grunted and abruptly stood.

Striding into the kitchen, he rummaged underneath the sink for a pan. Placing the pan in the sink, he turned on the faucet, ran his hand under the water and adjusted the valve for a warmer temperature. "Why were you already headed back?"

Caroline didn't answer him, but her fingers fretted at the bracelets on her wrist. He gritted his teeth. Her subconscious habit gouged at him.

He dumped half a carton of salt into the pan of water. Lifting the pan out of the sink, he carried it around the island to where she slumped on the sofa. As he knelt on the rug in front of her, some of the water sloshed over the sides of the pan. He settled the pan below her dangling feet.

"What are you doing?"

"Your feet are cut. The salt water's going to sting, but we've got to make sure we kill any bacterial infection."

She gulped. "I'm sorry, Weston. For yesterday. And for endangering Izzie. For putting her life in peril. Just like Jess—"

"You're nothing like her. I've told you that. And what happened today wasn't your fault. Izzie made her own ill-advised choices."

Taking hold of her ankles, he eased her feet into the pan. With a quick indrawn breath, she bit her lip. Twin dots of blood trembled on her bottom lip.

"I'm also sorry for yesterday." Her eyes glistened. "For everything."

Keeping one hand on her legs, he brushed the pad of his thumb across her mouth. "Everything?"

She closed her eyes and nestled her lips into his palm.

Weston's heart turned over in his chest. "Is sorry all you need to say to me, Caroline?"

Her startled gaze shot up to his. "No... I...I..."

Leaning over her, he removed the quilt from the couch and tucked its folds around her shaking body. He moved toward the kitchen. "You could change into one of my shirts." He extracted a dish towel from a drawer.

"I don't want your shirt, Weston."

Weston slung the towel across his shoulder. "What is it you do want, Caroline?" His eyes flared. "Really want? Tell me, because I don't know. And I want to know."

Time to face the truth. Weston deserved the truth. No more half-truths or mixed signals. No matter how hopeless everything was, Caroline respected him too much for anything less than total disclosure.

"I want you and Izzie and…" She flung wide her hands. "A life here with you, but—"

"But what?"

Her heart thudded. She had to make him see, to understand why it would be wrong for them to plan a life together. Wrong for him.

"I can't be the wife you deserve. I can't give you the children you want."

His eyes narrowed. "What are you talking about?"

"After what you went through with Jessica—"

"Is that what this has been about?" His face convulsed. "You are nothing like Jessica, Caroline."

She desperately wanted to not tell him. But only then could Weston gain closure. And be free to live the life he deserved. "When my father told me about my grandmother, I realized we could never be a family."

A line appeared between his brows. "What is

it exactly you think you know about your grand-mother? Are you sick?"

"Yes, I am."

His eyes widened. "Cancer, like your mother? Because if it is, I'm not about to let you face that without me."

"It's not cancer, but the diagnosis is as horri-ble and as incurable as what killed my mother."

Weston eased next to her on the sofa. "You told me about the past. There's nothing so terri-ble we couldn't handle it together." He took both her hands in his. "I love you, Caroline. Izzie loves you, too. For better or worse, we want to be there for you no matter what."

"But it would only be for worse, Weston. Don't you see?"

"No." He clenched his teeth. "I don't see."

"My grandmother battled depression until the day she finally took her own life. After my moth-er's death, the grief sent my father into a tailspin it took a decade for him to extricate himself from. I've inherited a predisposition for chronic depres-sion. A genetic curse."

She fretted at the bracelets until he frowned, and she dropped her hand. "I believed I'd fi-nally conquered the anxiety and depression. But now I realize there will be no getting well. Only stretches of time between breakdowns."

Caroline hardened her voice. "I won't put you

through that. And I'd never pass that terrible genetic weakness on to a child."

"I don't believe what happened to your grandmother will happen to you."

She stared at him. "You don't know that. None of us knows that."

"Exactly." He took hold of her hand. The bracelets jangled. "People were less accepting of depression in your grandmother's time. There were fewer resources."

He rubbed one of the beaded bracelets against her flesh. "She probably felt so alone. Never shared her struggles until she was in so deep she couldn't see a way out."

Caroline's gaze flitted to her hand in his. "But—"

"Your father is one of the best, strongest men I've ever known. Despite this dark enemy he battles, he lives a rich, full life." Weston threaded his fingers through hers. "You can live a rich, full life, too. You have friends. You have family. You have God."

A vein pulsed in his throat. "You can have me, too. Don't you understand how much I love you? I love you, with or without any potential children."

"You say that now." Her heart hammered. "But what about when I drag you and Izzie into the abyss with me?" Her mouth trembled. "I could never live with that."

"If you're so afraid…" He fingered the woven cord tied around her wrist. "Then why did you come back, Caroline?" His touch was featherlight against her scar.

The feel of his hand… The tender look in his eyes. Something broke in her heart.

"Because…" Tears cascaded down her face. "Because despite what my head tells me, my heart won't let me forget how much I love you, Weston."

In a way, it was freeing to finally say the words. And oddly enough, she felt free to breathe for the first time since her dad had told her about their family heritage.

Weston slipped off the couch and knelt once more at her feet. He draped the towel across his knees and moved aside the pan of water. Lifting her feet, he placed them in his lap. Tears dripped off her chin and plopped onto the towel in his hands. Gently, he dried first one foot and then the other. As if she were beloved, precious, cherished.

He held her barefoot in the palm of his hand. "I don't know what the future holds for anyone, Caroline. But what I've learned is that all any of us can do is face the future with trust in the One who holds us—our hopes, our dreams, our love and our lives—in the palm of His hand."

Weston ran his finger across the top of her foot. "The safest place we can rest. Secure in the knowledge in our faith that no matter what comes, He will somehow bring us through for our ultimate good."

His voice dropped to a whisper. "Because you, me, Izzie, we are His beloved, cherished, always precious children." He closed his eyes.

Praying for her, she realized. Praying for her as she struggled to come to terms with what she'd learned about herself and her family. Should she trust in Weston's love? Could she trust in a God who loved her that much?

Weston's eyes gleamed. "Give me a chance. Let me love you, Caroline."

Was it possible for someone like her? Truly possible? *Help me, God, to believe… To risk loving them and being loved.*

A silence hung suspended between them. A long moment fraught with fear, trembling hope and the possibility of unexpected joy.

She fell to her knees beside him. "Oh, Weston…" Her breath shuddered.

"Will you be my one true love, Caroline? Will you come home to me and stay with me forever?"

Her eyes never leaving his, one by one she removed the bracelets from her wrists. Allowing them to fall away onto the floor. "You are the one my heart's waited a lifetime to love."

Weston's face transformed, flooded with light and love. He leaned in—

Feet clomped on the stairs. "Have you asked her to marry us yet?" Izzie bellowed.

Smiling, Caroline imagined the little redhead hanging over the curving baluster of the railing.

Weston made a face, but his eyes twinkled in the lamplight. "Trying to, Monkey Girl, if you'll give me a chance," he yelled.

A loud, protracted sigh. "Well, hurry up, then."

Caroline smothered a laugh at his expression.

"Are you on one knee like they do in the movies, Daddy?"

Caroline arched her eyebrow. "What about it, Commander Clark?"

"You're enjoying this way too much." His lips grazed her earlobe.

She gave a delicious shiver.

Weston smirked at the lighthouse wall. "I think I can take things from here, Isabelle," he called.

"If you say so, Daddy. But please don't screw this up."

Weston sputtered, and Caroline gave in to the laughter.

"Just so you know, I had this really romantic beach picnic planned in my head," he growled.

"Since when?"

He pushed back his shoulders. "Since I kissed you on the Ferris wheel."

But Weston obligingly propped on one bended knee. "Caroline Victoria Duer, would you do me the honor of becoming my wife—" he glanced toward the wall "—and Izzie's mother?"

She captured his face between her hands and nodded.

He gave her that lopsided grin that tumbled her insides. "It doesn't count unless you say the word, Caroline."

The special word.

"Yes…" She smiled. "Yes, please."

And then he kissed her.

Epilogue

On the beach six weeks later, Caroline scanned the ocean waves off the lighthouse point. With the cottage lights darkened, she, Izzie and Weston waited for Turtle Mama to emerge.

She glanced over to Weston stretched out beside her on the beach towel. Legs extended, he leaned back on his elbows, his face upturned to the moonlight.

"Wake me when Turtle Mama gets here, Turtle Lady."

"Hush, Daddy," Izzie hissed, sitting cross-legged between them.

Caroline stifled a laugh. "Yeah, Daddy…"

His eyes opened and he sat up. Wrapping his arm around Caroline's waist, he tugged her closer. "I'm not your daddy."

"No." She kissed his chin. "You're not. You are my heart's desire."

"Shhh…" Izzie rounded her eyes at them both. His smile fluttered Caroline's insides.

"Better enjoy the silence," he whispered in her ear. "Egg laying is about the only time we can get your new daughter to stop talking." His mouth brushed across Caroline's earlobe.

Caroline giggled, which earned another glare from Izzie. Her brand-new, beloved daughter. As for her brand-new husband? Life with Weston was more wonderful than she could've imagined.

She'd surprised and pleased Weston by not wanting to wait more than a few weeks to get married. Which, Honey mock-complained, put her and Amelia in a bind if they were going to throw together the wedding of Caroline's dreams.

But her dreams were simple. Her dream had already come true in this man now at her side. Still, she thought her heart would burst from joy when her father walked her down the clamshell path to where Reverend Parks and Weston awaited. Another dream realized, the restoration of a relationship with her father.

In a white sheath dress that trailed in the sand, she and Weston pledged their love for each other forever on the lawn beneath the towering lighthouse amid the sounds of the surf crashing on the rocks below.

Her sisters acted as her bridesmaids. Her brothers-in-law stood as Weston's groomsmen. Izzie had her big moment in a frilly sundress as she scattered flower petals to the wind. Max served as ring bearer—when he wasn't chipping seashells into the ocean.

Caroline had been nervous meeting Weston's parents for the first time. But his mother had taken Caroline aside at the rehearsal dinner.

"Thank you for loving my son," his mother whispered with tears in her eyes. "And for loving Izzie, too. I was so afraid he'd never allow himself to love anyone ever again. That he'd always be alone."

But it was Caroline who was grateful. Grateful for Weston loving her. Grateful most of all to God for the second chance He'd given them to love each other and Him.

She'd come full circle. Back to the most enduring of family legacies—her heritage of faith. Back somehow where she'd begun. Home on the Eastern Shore of Virginia. Reconnected with her family and, of all things, a mom. A title she'd never imagined could be hers.

As for the future? She faced each new dawn hand in hand with God. *Praise God, from whom every blessing flows.*

It was quite a party afterward with their Kiptohanock friends, church family and Roland, her new boss at the Kiptohanock Marine Rescue Center.

A smile tugged at her lips as she thought of that splendid day only a month ago. Sweet tea, hush puppies and beach music. Nothing better. A real Eastern Shore–style celebration.

Something glimmered on an incoming wave.

"Look, Izzie." She gestured toward the sea creature slowly rising from beneath the foaming surf. "Turtle Mama has returned to lay her final eggs for the season. We probably won't see her again for a few years. But when it's time, she'll come home."

Izzie wormed her way into somehow being in both Caroline's and Weston's laps. "Like us." She let out a sigh of contentment that Caroline could feel all the way to her own toes.

She kissed the top of Izzie's red head. "Yes, Ladybug."

Weston hugged both his ladies. "Home just like us."

* * * * *

*If you loved this tale of sweet romance,
pick up these other stories from
author Lisa Carter:*

*COAST GUARD COURTSHIP
COAST GUARD SWEETHEART*

Available now from Love Inspired!

*Find more great reads at
www.LoveInspired.com*

Dear Reader,

Years ago, a teacher friend gave me a nautilus shell. This friend struggled against the darkness and battled sadness, but told no one. Tragically, one day he chose to end his life. I've since pondered the meaning behind the unique design of the nautilus. This story is an outgrowth of that takeaway. I believe it is important to talk about depression to combat the lie that we are alone. I hope this story illustrates the truth that it's okay to ask for help. Life is often hard, but God is always good.

Like King David, the prophet Elijah and the Apostle Paul, Caroline struggles with depression. She grapples with the implications of her family heritage. If Caroline's story describes your current situation, I pray you will seek the advice of a medical professional and wise, spiritual counsel, too, so that you might take partake of the richer, fuller, abundant life God desires for you to experience. Life is worth living.

During the writing of this story, I've cared for my aging father, who suffered with advanced Alzheimer's, and I've pondered the legacy I will one day leave my children. My father's homegoing occurred on February 12, 2016. I don't know what the future holds for you or for me. But I've learned that I must trust in the God who holds us—our hopes, our dreams, our loved ones and our lives—in the palm of His hand. The safest place we can rest.

Why? Because you and I, we are His beloved, cherished, always precious children. Ultimately, a heritage of faith is the best legacy I've inherited from my family. Like the multichambered nautilus, I hope the cross section of your past will encourage you as to how far you've traveled. And inspire you as to how far you may yet go.

I hope you have enjoyed taking this journey with me, Caroline and Weston. I would also love to hear from you. You may email me at lisa@lisacarterauthor.com or visit www.lisacarterauthor.com.

Wishing you fair winds and following seas,
Lisa Carter

LARGER-PRINT BOOKS!

**GET 2 FREE
LARGER-PRINT NOVELS
PLUS 2 FREE
MYSTERY GIFTS**

Love Inspired®

SUSPENSE
RIVETING INSPIRATIONAL ROMANCE

Larger-print novels are now available...

YES! Please send me 2 FREE LARGER-PRINT Love Inspired® Suspense novels and my 2 FREE mystery gifts (gifts are worth about $10). After receiving them, if I don't wish to receive any more books, I can return the shipping statement marked "cancel." If I don't cancel, I will receive 4 brand-new novels every month and be billed just $5.49 per book in the U.S. or $5.99 per book in Canada. That's a savings of at least 19% off the cover price. It's quite a bargain! Shipping and handling is just 50¢ per book in the U.S. and 75¢ per book in Canada.* I understand that accepting the 2 free books and gifts places me under no obligation to buy anything. I can always return a shipment and cancel at any time. Even if I never buy another book, the two free books and gifts are mine to keep forever.

110/310 IDN GH6P

Name _____ (PLEASE PRINT)

Address _____ Apt. #

City _____ State/Prov. _____ Zip/Postal Code

Signature (if under 18, a parent or guardian must sign)

Mail to the **Reader Service**:
IN U.S.A.: P.O. Box 1867, Buffalo, NY 14240-1867
IN CANADA: P.O. Box 609, Fort Erie, Ontario L2A 5X3

**Are you a current subscriber to Love Inspired® Suspense books
and want to receive the larger-print edition?
Call 1-800-873-8635 or visit www.ReaderService.com.**

* Terms and prices subject to change without notice. Prices do not include applicable taxes. Sales tax applicable in N.Y. Canadian residents will be charged applicable taxes. Offer not valid in Quebec. This offer is limited to one order per household. Not valid for current subscribers to Love Inspired Suspense larger-print books. All orders subject to credit approval. Credit or debit balances in a customer's account(s) may be offset by any other outstanding balance owed by or to the customer. Please allow 4 to 6 weeks for delivery. Offer available while quantities last.

Your Privacy—The Reader Service is committed to protecting your privacy. Our Privacy Policy is available online at www.ReaderService.com or upon request from the Reader Service.

We make a portion of our mailing list available to reputable third parties that offer products we believe may interest you. If you prefer that we not exchange your name with third parties, or if you wish to clarify or modify your communication preferences, please visit us at www.ReaderService.com/consumerchoice or write to us at Reader Service Preference Service, P.O. Box 9062, Buffalo, NY 14240-9062. Include your complete name and address.

LISLP15

REQUEST YOUR FREE BOOKS!
2 FREE WHOLESOME ROMANCE NOVELS
IN LARGER PRINT
PLUS 2
FREE
MYSTERY GIFTS

☀☀☀☀☀☀☀☀☀☀☀☀☀☀☀☀☀☀☀☀☀☀☀☀

HEARTWARMING™
❅❅❅❅❅❅❅❅❅❅❅❅❅❅❅❅❅❅❅❅❅❅❅

Wholesome, tender romances

YES! Please send me 2 FREE Harlequin® Heartwarming Larger-Print novels and my 2 FREE mystery gifts (gifts worth about $10). After receiving them, if I don't wish to receive any more books, I can return the shipping statement marked "cancel." If I don't cancel, I will receive 4 brand-new larger-print novels every month and be billed just $5.24 per book in the U.S. or $5.99 per book in Canada. That's a savings of at least 19% off the cover price. It's quite a bargain! Shipping and handling is just 50¢ per book in the U.S. and 75¢ per book in Canada.* I understand that accepting the 2 free books and gifts places me under no obligation to buy anything. I can always return a shipment and cancel at any time. Even if I never buy another book, the two free books and gifts are mine to keep forever.

161/361 IDN GHX2

Name _____ (PLEASE PRINT) _____

Address _____ Apt. # ____

City _____ State/Prov. _____ Zip/Postal Code ____

Signature (if under 18, a parent or guardian must sign)

Mail to the **Reader Service:**
IN U.S.A.: P.O. Box 1867, Buffalo, NY 14240-1867
IN CANADA: P.O. Box 609, Fort Erie, Ontario L2A 5X3

* Terms and prices subject to change without notice. Prices do not include applicable taxes. Sales tax applicable in N.Y. Canadian residents will be charged applicable taxes. Offer not valid in Quebec. This offer is limited to one order per household. Not valid for current subscribers to Harlequin Heartwarming larger-print books. All orders subject to credit approval. Credit or debit balances in a customer's account(s) may be offset by any other outstanding balance owed by or to the customer. Please allow 4 to 6 weeks for delivery. Offer available while quantities last.

Your Privacy—The Reader Service is committed to protecting your privacy. Our Privacy Policy is available online at www.ReaderService.com or upon request from the Reader Service.

We make a portion of our mailing list available to reputable third parties that offer products we believe may interest you. If you prefer that we not exchange your name with third parties, or if you wish to clarify or modify your communication preferences, please visit us at www.ReaderService.com/consumerchoice or write to us at Reader Service Preference Service, P.O. Box 9062, Buffalo, NY 14240-9062. Include your complete name and address.

HW15

WESTERN (WP) PROMISES

YES! Please send me **The Western Promises Collection** in Larger Print. This collection begins with 3 FREE books and 2 FREE gifts (gifts valued at approx. $14.00 retail) in the first shipment, along with the other first 4 books from the collection! If I do not cancel, I will receive 8 monthly shipments until I have the entire 51-book Western Promises collection. I will receive 2 or 3 FREE books in each shipment and I will pay just $4.99 US/ $5.89 CDN for each of the other four books in each shipment, plus $2.99 for shipping and handling per shipment. *If I decide to keep the entire collection, I'll have paid for only 32 books, because 19 books are FREE! I understand that accepting the 3 free books and gifts places me under no obligation to buy anything. I can always return a shipment and cancel at any time. My free books and gifts are mine to keep no matter what I decide.

272 HCN 3070 472 HCN 3070

Name	(PLEASE PRINT)	
Address		Apt. #
City	State/Prov.	Zip/Postal Code
Signature (if under 18, a parent or guardian must sign)		

Mail to the **Reader Service:**
IN U.S.A.: P.O. Box 1867, Buffalo, NY 14240-1867
IN CANADA: P.O. Box 609, Fort Erie, Ontario L2A 5X3

* Terms and prices subject to change without notice. Prices do not include applicable taxes. Sales tax applicable in N.Y. Canadian residents will be charged applicable taxes. This offer is limited to one order per household. All orders subject to approval. Credit or debit balances in a customer's account(s) may be offset by any other outstanding balance owed by or to the customer. Please allow 4 to 6 weeks for delivery. Offer available while quantities last. Offer not available to Quebec residents.

Your Privacy—The Reader Service is committed to protecting your privacy. Our Privacy Policy is available online at www.ReaderService.com or upon request from the Reader Service.

We make a portion of our mailing list available to reputable third parties that offer products we believe may interest you. If you prefer that we not exchange your name with third parties, or if you wish to clarify or modify your communication preferences, please visit us at www.ReaderService.com/consumerschoice or write to us at Reader Service Preference Service, P.O. Box 9062, Buffalo, NY 14240-9062. Include your complete name and address.

READERSERVICE.COM

Manage your account online!

- Review your order history
- Manage your payments
- Update your address

---

*We've designed the
Reader Service website
just for you.*

Enjoy all the features!

- Discover new series available to you,
  and read excerpts from any series.
- Respond to mailings and special
  monthly offers.
- Connect with favorite authors at
  the blog.
- Browse the Bonus Bucks catalog
  and online-only exculsives.
- Share your feedback.

Visit us at:
ReaderService.com